ADITYA N

Until Love Sets Us Apart

To Love with Love

FiNGERPRINT!

Published 2024

FiNGERPRINT!
An imprint of Prakash Books India Pvt. Ltd

113/A, Darya Ganj,
New Delhi-110 002
Email: info@prakashbooks.com/sales@prakashbooks.com

Fingerprint Publishing
@FingerprintP
@fingerprintpublishingbooks
www.fingerprintpublishing.com

Copyright © 2018 Prakash Books India Pvt. Ltd.
Copyright Text © Aditya Nighhot

This is a work of fiction. Names, characters, places and incidents are either product of the author's imagination or are used fictitiously, and any resemblance to any actual person, living or dead, events or locales is purely coincidental.

All rights reserved. No part of this publication may be reproduced, stored in a retrieval system or transmitted in any form or by any means, electronic, mechanical, photocopying, recording or otherwise (except for mentions in reviews or edited excerpts in the media) without the written permission of the publisher.

ISBN: 978 93 8814 425 4

Everything is fair in love and war . . .
and this is love with war

ALSO BY THE AUTHOR

TAGGED FOR LIFE: WILL YOU BE MY WIFE?
Reviews

Captivating, engrossing & heart-wrenching, Tagged for Life is a must-buy book.

Times of India

The book deserves all the love and is a must for every bookshelf.

India Today

Aditya's unique writing style will make you thirst for more.

Yahoo News

The new-age romance author has given this book his all.

Republic India

Tagged for life has to definitely be on your bucket list

JIO News

Worth every read!

Indian Express

From the first page to the last, the writing hooks you immediately and makes it a page turner.

Business Standard

Nighhot as always has delivered his best.

Lokmat Times

No wonder, the book is a bestseller!

Maharashtra Portal

Aditya Nighhot's writing brings the characters to life, making readers emotionally invested in their journey.

The Literary Lounge Express

UNHOOKED & UNBOOKED
Reviews

3 most loved book of the year.
ANI

He engages us in his riveting tale of two couples who have completely different and opposite beliefs from each other.
The Print

One of the best Romance Authors of India, Dr. Aditya R. Nighhot has been in the limelight with his books.
Republic News India

Aditya's books have been popular not only among the youth but have also collected praises from the critics.
The Telegraph News

The book tells a story that is completely relatable to our generation.
Business Standard

U N ME...IT'S COMPLICATED
Reviews

A must-read book for every student who is struggling to achieve their goals.
The Asian Chronicle

A modern day love story!
Thinkerviews.com

What an intriguing story! The focus of U n Me...It's Complicated seems to be romance but as the story unfurls it becomes clear that it is much more about self discovery and coping up with relationships.
bookishelf

CONTENTS

Acknowledgements   *9*
Prologue   *11*

1. How It All Began   **15**
2. We Had to Be Friends!   **44**
3. Love Is Life   **71**
4. One Step Closer   **88**
5. Can't Live Without You   **101**
6. Winning Is Not Everything!   **114**
7. Meeting the Parents   **138**
8. In the Blink of an Eye   **160**
9. We Want Justice!   **177**
10. I Want You Back!   **197**
11. Payback Time!   **202**
12. Finally, We See Rohit!   **212**

Epilogue   *223*
Author's Thoughts, Reader's Verdict!   *226*
The Book Says   *230*
About the Author   *231*

Acknowledgements

Big thank you to all my readers who have been supporting this book and have helped it achieve "The Best Romance Book of the Year" award. Any piece of art is always incomplete without a few helping hands. I would like to thank some of the key people involved in the making of this book without whom the book would be incomplete:

- God for His blessings—without Him almost everything would be incomplete.
- My parents, for their constant support through thick and thin and for showering their blessings upon me.
- Special mention: Sakina Fatehnagri, Ketan Vaidya, and Sameer Inamdar for being my first readers and helping me throughout the making of this book.

- My cousins Digvijay Chavan, Chaitanya Nighot, and Namrata Gawade for helping me reach out to my initial readers with my debut novel and thereby actually making me a published author.
- My maternal grandparents for their eternal love and my late paternal grandfather who would have been so happy with my success if he were here today. I am sure he is looking down at me from heaven and is bestowing his blessings upon me.
- Shikha Sabharwal, Pooja Dadwal, my editor Vidya Sury, Surina Jain, Neeraj Chawla, and the entire team at Fingerprint! Publishing and Prakash Books for taking my published book a step ahead.
- Mr. Suhail Mathur and the team of The Book Bakers literary agency for their support and advice.
- Each and every friend and relative who has always supported and motivated me—love you all. Apologies if I have missed out mentioning anyone in particular—it is completely unintentional.

Special mention to every reader for their unflinching love and for always supporting me and accepting me as an author. Big thanks to you and my extended family on all social networking platforms.

Prologue

The car took a dangerously sharp turn, its tyres screeching. Just as they passed the main road, the sound of its horn reached a crescendo, with the driver changing gears and speeding like there was no tomorrow. As the tension mounted, they broke out in cold sweat and fear gripped them. As the driver's palms steered the wheel, the tears poured down his face. He was miserable and his heart felt like it was about to shatter into a million pieces. Sitting beside him, Alok desperately hoped for the best outcome. He wished nothing had happened and recalled all the Godly idols he could think of. They had no inkling of what had happened at the other end—yet the uncertainty drove them to pray with every ounce of faith they could muster. The trepidation could kill them any moment. With tears flowing down their cheeks, they felt their lives had come to a dead end—just like a road ends. But theirs had a no U-turn board that would bring them back to safety!

It was ironic that just a few minutes ago, the clock struck 11:00 and the moonlight fell upon them. Its effulgence had made it a perfect night to sit on the terrace with a friend, look up at the dark sky, get drunk, sing songs, remember the best moments of their lives, and admire the twinkling stars, which shone down on them. They were happy until the worst nightmare struck them.

How predictable our lives are! It is a new day on the calendar for each one of us, but in reality, it is just the same as the previous one. You get up at a fixed time, brush your teeth with the same tooth brush, take a shower, and grab the morning bus or drive yourself to college or your workplace. There, you have that fixed margin of time before you actually attend your college lectures or begin your work. Then you go to the same cafeteria and have the same breakfast. Work begins as usual with the same thoughts in your head, musing over your purpose in this place; you then habitually shrug those thoughts off. You certainly are not alone, wherever you are. Enter, your friends and sometimes, even your girlfriend or your boyfriend. The same bunch of people and the nonsense chatter and things you do with them are the only things that actually keep on changing every day. The day goes on as it usually does—no fuss, no surprises—*just the same old routine* as many would say.

Predictability has become the backbone of your life. You can foretell upcoming events or situations. But in some sense, you find it very comforting when every day is the same. You assume you are in charge and think your life is very much under your control, little realising that fate is actually a bitch. While your life seems picture perfect, it plays its little tricks on you. It has its own game, its own players, its own umpire, and its own rules. It is playing the game against you and you can do nothing—for you are reduced to being a mere spectator who actually knows nothing of what is coming next.

Sometimes, we appreciate the small tricks it plays on us and keep reminding ourselves with the two golden words 'THINK POSITIVE.' But what if the same trick is so cruel that it takes away all the positivity within you? What if the patience, the determination, and the dedication you had developed over the years to fight back any difficulty get lost in a void of pain? Our predictable life comes crashing down like a house of cards. Everything that you had planned, every dream that had been fulfilled gets snatched away from you and your life plunges into a deep abyss named 'CHAOS.'

CHAPTER 1

How It All Began

"This one is for Aadi," said Nikhil, raising his glass.

Not wine or alcohol but a glass which contained iced tea. My friends and I were sitting in one of the restaurants near my college. I was giving them a treat post my first novel release. Well, not actually a release! 'Print' would be a better word! So, following the five hundred odd copies that I had distributed amongst my friends and relatives, I was rejoicing over the positive response I had received. They had liked it and here I was, partying with my friends. I introduced Nikhil and Varun to the others which included Naineesh, Hrushikesh, and Ajinkya, friends from my new college.

"When I was working on my first novel, I really didn't have the confidence in myself and never believed that it would ever turn out to be so good," I said, offering some pizza to Naineesh.

"Yeah, after all some credit has to be given to us!" both Nikhil and Varun boasted. Everyone burst into laughter, looking at their expressions.

"Aadi always speaks about the two of you," said Naineesh, grabbing some garlic bread.

"I have to give them credit; it's because of them I actually thought about writing," I said with a smile.

"Dude, that makes us look small!" remarked Varun.

Everyone smiled. We then spoke about our college lives—how our day began and how it ended. All of us were medical college students, and found our course to be the most difficult one. Nikhil had just finished his twelfth standard and was waiting for the results to be declared.

"How's everything going between Saisha and you, Varun?" asked Ajinkya. "Only if you don't mind sharing it, because we got a hint of your relationship in Aadi's novel and I am curious to know about what's going on in your life," he added.

"At the best phase, I can say," replied Varun.

"Oh! So, perfect *jodi*, huh? God bless you both," joked Hrushikesh.

"Thank you, Hrushikesh," replied Varun with a huge smile on his face.

"Let's click some selfies," said Nikhil, turning on his mobile camera.

All of us went through the photo sessions, forgetting the food on the table.

"Have you been working on any novel lately?" Varun asked me.

"I want to, but I am unable to zero in on a good story—rather I can't think of one," I replied, scratching my head.

"Think, dude. You are so filmy, I am sure you will get one," mocked Naineesh, laughing.

"Oh, c'mon you're still filmy? Don't tell me!" exclaimed Nikhil.

"He is! And way too much!" added Ajinkya, giving some impetus to the conversation.

Nikhil, Varun, and I had not met one another for months and so they hardly knew anything about my new life. I was responsible for the long gap as I had become rather busy.

"Hang on, I'll go pay the bill," I said, making an excuse.

"Look, he's running out of conversation," Nikhil teased me as the others laughed.

I ignored them and walked to the counter, paid the bill, and joined my friends back at the table.

"There's big news coming right from the police. The murderer has been caught today by the Pune Police Department," announced the news reporter on the news channel.

My head turned towards the screen as I paid attention to what was being broadcast. I was intrigued.

"Shhh . . . Please look," I signalled my friends to lower their voices and pointed towards the television screen.

"An MBBS student who was found guilty for murdering four people and who has been missing has now been caught by the Pune Police. He was tracked down by the police and was found near the Pune district court. He is now in police custody," the reporter continued.

"Oooo . . . C'mon, how can an MBBS student turn into a murderer, all of a sudden!" exclaimed Ajinkya.

"Who said all of a sudden? Maybe he had a cruel mind or maybe circumstances turned him into a murderer," replied Naineesh.

We looked at one another and then turned to the television screen again. Naturally, we were all interested in the news as it was something related to our own field—medicine.

"The police say that the guilty student didn't try to harm them although he did try to escape. We were informed that in order to stop him, ACP Deshmukh fired a bullet, just below his right knee cap, capturing him. He will first be taken to the hospital and then to the police station. The police refused to disclose any further details. Our next news is . . ."

"Here's my next story," I said, pointing towards the screen.

"What? A story about a murderer? Why are you poking your nose into a criminal case?" asked Nikhil, shocked.

"Don't mess with criminal cases. He is a murderer!" added Varun.

"But he is also a doctor—what we all are going to become in the next few years. And anyway, looking at him,

I don't think he was a professional killer or a person who would murder someone for his own greed," I replied.

"How can you be so sure?" Hrushikesh asked me, curiously.

"Just instinct . . . I have no reason for it," I replied.

"You might be wrong!" added Naineesh, as we all headed towards our bikes.

As I sat on my bike, I said, "I think I should give it a go. Here's what I'll do: I will interview the accused, collect data from the police, and frame everything into a novel. My gut feeling tells me there's more to his life, perhaps an unhappy past. If I turn out to be wrong, I'll just give up my plan."

"Hmm . . . sounds interesting, especially the interview thing. I'm in; let's go together, what say?" Nikhil added.

"Give me a high-five then," I smiled. With an unusual sparkle in my eyes, I was filled with excitement and felt my confidence rise. I had stretched out of my comfort zone. This was something challenging and I was overjoyed to start something new.

1 August 2015 - At the Police Station

"Are you sure we should be dealing with this?" Nikhil asked me as we reached the police station.

"Don't worry, Nikhil. It's going to be fine, c'mon let's go in," I replied.

We took deep breaths to compose ourselves. The police station was crowded and we felt as if we had entered into some kind of fish market. No one seemed to pay attention when we made our entry. We waited for a while, wondering where and how to start our inquiry. The entrance was small but tidy. A few jeeps were parked outside. Inside, it was noisy, with the policemen busy in their work. The constant ringing of the telephone made the loudest noise. Although a couple of visitors were sitting on the benches inside, the *chaiwala* was the most frequent visitor.

"Hmm, *bola kay kam ahe*? (Speak up, what work do you have?)," a policeman asked us as we approached him. He was going through some files when I managed to read his name tag which read 'A. Tambe.' I realised he was a sub-inspector from the number of stars on his uniform. His potbelly was prominent. Though his shirt was tucked into the waistband of his trousers, his belt was so loose that it looked like it could fall off any moment. His lips were red with the paan or *supari* he seemed to be habitually chewing. Not bothering to offer us a seat, he went on, "*Arey bolo na kya kam hai*? (What work do you have?)"

"Good morning, sir, my name is Aditya. Sir, I wanted to enquire about the recent murder case involving the doctor . . ." I had barely completed my sentence but found I had already spoken enough to draw the sub-inspector's attention.

For the first time since we entered, he looked up from his files, tilted his head sideways, and stared at us suspiciously, scaring the hell out of Nikhil. He elbowed me and the next moment found me hurriedly telling the officer that I wanted to write a book based on the accused's case and to do this, I needed his help to interview the person. I was as polite as possible and sat down, even though the sub-inspector didn't offer me a chair.

"*Tumhi patrakar ka?* (Are you a news reporter?) You are not allowed here now," he replied, switching from Marathi to his vernacular English.

"Sir, I am not a news reporter. I am an author and also a medical student. I just want to write about the case and I need your support to get some information."

"*Sahebanchi* permission *lagel*. (I will have to take permission from the senior officer)," he said carelessly, while sipping some water from his bottle and turning a few pages of the file he was going through.

"So, when can we meet him?" asked Nikhil, directly.

"He is busy today, come tomorrow," he replied, clearly not interested in entertaining us.

We got up and walked out. Somewhere deep inside, I was filled with a sense of satisfaction. This approach somehow made me feel that we had made some progress. With mixed emotions—happy that the meeting was possible and disappointed about being told to wait—we headed back home.

Over the next few days, Nikhil and I visited the police station every day, but nothing worthwhile happened. Almost a fortnight passed and we began to lose hope. Disappointed, I wondered whether I should ditch the plan. We were low for a couple of days and this was enough for Varun to guess what was annoying us. Right from our junior college days, he had always been able to judge our mood and the reason behind it. He also knew how to get us back on track and threw a mini party at his place. Like the old days we were in his room watching our favourite movie, accompanied by snacks we enjoyed. While Nikhil and Varun were seated comfortably, I was restless, fidgeting with the Rubik's Cube that one would always find on Varun's table. Oblivious to the joy of re-living our old days, I was so lost in my own world that I didn't realise that someone's shadow was blocking the light. I looked up to see Varun's dad standing there and got up to greet him. His presence, for some reason, made me feel suddenly optimistic. He joined us and we paused the movie. He offered to play a game of cards with us. This was a little unusual but his company was rare, so we readily agreed. We started playing and uncle began to narrate anecdotes from his school days, about his friends, and the fun he had with them. He mentioned that the phase of life we were in was the best and we should make the most of it. He was nostalgic over how his friends and he had parted ways to become something in life. He was also happy for one of his friends, ACP Deshmukh, who had recently been transferred to our city. On hearing this, I looked up instantaneously. I knew that ACP Deshmukh was in charge of the case. I felt as though my face was divided into parts, each with a different expression. Surprise, joy, and misery. I couldn't resist sharing my interest in the case with Varun's dad. And what happened next was nothing short of a miracle. Varun's father agreed to help and fixed up a meeting for me. I was on top of the world. I thanked Varun and his parents profusely.

24 August 2015

Varun, Nikhil, and I reached the police station well before time. We were asked to wait for a while as the officer was busy. After an hour we were asked to head to the officer's cabin.

While entering the cabin, we made a special effort to read the name plate outside, which read ACP R. Deshmukh.

Both Varun and Mr. Deshmukh greeted each other in an informal way and then Varun introduced us. We were offered a seat. Mr. Deshmukh appeared to be in his mid-forties. He was of dusky complexion, with an excellent physique. His smart attire added to his attractive personality, giving the impression that he could not be easily outwitted. We told him the reason for our visit and what we wanted.

"*Dekho*, interview with the accused is little difficult at present, but you may try again after a few days. Keeping safety issues in consideration and to avoid evidence from being contaminated before the jury's decision, there are rules which don't allow strangers to meet the accused. At the same time his violence also imposes a threat, so I can't really allow you there," ACP R. Deshmukh said.

We asked him if there was any other way but he brushed our requests aside and repeated that we try again after some months. We felt disappointed but were left with no other option.

"Sir, can you tell us about the person? Only if you don't have a problem," I asked the officer.

"Well, I really don't want to disappoint you, so I will

try but it would be brief, as I am very busy at the moment with some of the other cases I am dealing with," he replied, folding his hands and leaning back in his chair.

He then rang the bell to call one of his attendants.

"Sawant, *char chaha aana* (Sawant, bring four cups of tea)," he ordered and added, "Special one!"

ACP R. Deshmukh began to talk.

15 May 2015

It was my first day in Pune after I was transferred from Mumbai. I received a warm welcome. The former officer, ACP Mr. Lokhande, handed over the charge of the jurisdiction to me, after the department celebrated his farewell with mixed emotions. He was transferred to Amravati, far from Pune.

After I settled in my cabin, I called my staff inside for a quick round of briefing. They filled me in on the regions that came under my jurisdiction.

"A brutal murder case has made the situation pretty tense since the past few days," Inspector Bhosale told me, after I asked about on-going cases.

He placed the FIR in front of me and continued, "*Saheb*, recently the son of a businessman was murdered. His name was Rohan Khanna."

"When did this happen?" I asked him as I was going through the FIR statement given by Rohan Khanna's parents.

"On the tenth of May, sir," he replied.

"That is five days back," I remarked.

"Yes, sir," replied Inspector Bhosale.

"Rohan's body was found at his residence. Investigations showed that he was alone at home when he was murdered. On inspecting his body, we found wounds and scars which suggested some sort of struggle. The whole bedroom was a mess. There was blood everywhere, things were shattered, mirror and glasses and a chair broken into pieces. The chair had a rope wound around it, which suggested that Rohan had been tied there for a while. His body appeared as though he had been tortured before being killed. His head and face had severe injuries where glass pieces were embedded. This could have happened from being banged on the mirror and hit with various glass objects. His body showed signs of a knife being stabbed several times with great force," Inspector Bhosale continued briefing me.

I took a deep breath, imagining the scene enough to get goose bumps.

After a long pause, I asked, "Any progress in finding the murderer?"

"No, sir, even after interrogations around the neighbourhood, we couldn't get any eyewitnesses. Whoever he is, he is a monster and has a cruel mind, sir."

"We need to find him immediately, Bhosale," I said firmly, getting up from my chair.

"Yes, sir, we will definitely find him," he replied in a promising voice and continued, "Sir, the same day another murder took place in Koregaon Park. A body was found in a Honda City car, shot to death. A part of his skull had been chipped off; the blood was splattered on the window and the windshield. We were lucky to find his driving license and get his personal information. The person shot dead was Suraj Dixit. The shots were at close range. The glass being intact, the murderer was probably in the car."

"Didn't anyone see the murder? Any witnesses?" I asked.

"No, sir, again no eyewitnesses. The car was parked under a tree, near a dead end; nobody heard the gunshot as there aren't any residential areas nearby."

"What was Suraj doing there?"

"We don't know, sir. On checking the vehicle and Suraj's body, we found no signs of fight or resistance. All we found was a gun in his car. To everybody's surprise, the twist in the story is that the gun was issued in the name of Rohan Khanna. It was his personal gun."

"What!" I exclaimed. "So, there is a possibility that he might have murdered Suraj," I continued.

"We thought the same, sir. On inquiry, we came to know that Suraj and Rohan were friends. The fact that there were no signs of fight or resistance in the car strengthened our assumptions, until the post-mortem reports arrived. They said that Rohan's death occurred a few minutes prior to Suraj's death."

"That makes it even clearer. There is a common murderer between the two. How far is Koregaon Park from Rohan's house?" I went on.

"Two kilometres, sir."

"And one thing, sir, I forgot to mention," continued

Bhosale, "Suraj had received a call from Rohan's mobile, at about 5.30 in the evening on the same day. Rohan's death occurred around 5.45 p.m. and Suraj's death around 6.15 p.m."

I took some time to think, drank a glass of water, and said, "There can be two suppositions:

A) Rohan knew that there was a threat to their lives and called Suraj.

or

B) Rohan called Suraj when the murderer was present there, only because he was compelled to do so.

I went through the files and checked Rohan's and Suraj's personal information.

- Both were pursuing B.Sc. and studied in the same college.
- Both were twenty-two years old, Rohan being a month older than Suraj.

"Let's go to Rohan's house, take two policemen with us," I ordered, getting up from my chair.

Within the next half an hour, we reached Rohan's house.

"Any news about the murderer, sir?" asked Rohan's father, worried, as we stepped inside their house.

"No, sir, we are working on it. Please co-operate with us; we want to re-investigate this place," replied Inspector Bhosale.

With a negative response from our end, Rohan's mother burst out into tears. I felt sorry for her.

"He was my only son. What will I do without him? How should I live?" she sobbed.

I tried to reassure her that we would find the guilty as soon as we could, but that didn't really help change the situation.

Our profession is one of those where we are supposed to punish the guilty but situations punish the innocents beforehand. As human beings, our hearts ache too, but we have to keep our emotions aside, as our profession demands it. Hardening our hearts, we entered into Rohan's bedroom, the scene of the crime. Although the room was clean and everything in its proper place, Inspector Bhosale briefed me about the scene for the second time. I looked for clues, just in case the murderer had left any. I checked the drawers, his cupboard, and then had a word with his parents and the maid, to find out about their whereabouts when the crime had taken place. There was no one in the house that day. I was a bit astonished by their answers.

To confirm certain things, I asked the maid to bring me a glass of water. When she brought it, I asked her to place it on the table. Later, I picked up the glass of water with my gloves on, discarded the water into the sink and bagged the glass to hand over to the forensic department to examine for fingerprints. We already had Rohan's shirt and watch in our custody, all we needed was to check if the fingerprints on the glass matched with the ones on his shirt.

"Where is Rohan's mobile?" I asked Bhosale.

"Sir, it has been missing. We tried tracking it through GPS but the mobile is unreachable since the day of the crime. It is the same with Suraj's mobile. We tried tracking them, but failed, and it seems the SIM card has been removed from the device. We can track the murderer once he or she turns the handsets on," he replied.

"It is definitely a man's work, going by the brutality of it," I replied in a confident voice.

"Where were they last traced?" I asked Inspector Bhosale.

"At Koregaon Park, sir. After murdering Suraj, he probably removed the SIM card and switched off the mobile phones."

Then again, I was only physically present out there but mentally in the deepest level of my thinking zone. I was completely clueless of what to do next. I searched through one of his drawers and found a photo. There were three boys in the photo. On the extreme left was Suraj and on the extreme right was Rohan, with an unknown face in the middle. I asked Rohan's parents about the unknown person and discovered that he was Rohan's friend, Ajay. I inquired about his whereabouts and noted down his contact number. I then told Bhosale to call the number but he came up saying that the number was switched off.

"What are you thinking, sir?" he continued.

"There can again be two possibilities:

A)   Ajay is the third one to be murdered.

OR

B) He himself is the murderer.

There is something in common between the three of them."

Meanwhile, Inspector Bhosale received a call from the control room.

After the call ended, he came up to me and said, "Saheb, Suraj's mobile was switched on five minutes ago and a call has been made to an unknown number."

"Where was the mobile last traced?" I asked increasing my pace and walking out of the house.

"Sir, at Swargate, and it is still there," Bhosale responded promptly, following me.

"Send a police team immediately to that location," I ordered as we got into the car.

"What was the conversation that took place between the two?" I continued.

"Sir, the murderer instructed the person he called to meet him and not to attend calls from any unknown number. It seems that they have had a conversation before, on some another number."

"Hmm, probably. Trace the number now. I am sure it's Ajay who was at the other end."

Bhosale turned on the GPS and said, "Sir, the person who was at the other end is heading towards Sinhagad road."

I immediately asked the driver to head there. Sinhagad road was at the opposite end from our location. Swargate, where the Suraj's mobile was tracked, came midway and Katraj came next, which was where Ajay lived. Sinhagad road was a few kilometres away from Katraj. It was difficult for us to reach there in time, so I asked the driver to hurry up.

"Keep tracking the person who was at the other end; let's assume it is Ajay," I ordered Inspector Bhosale.

"Sir, he has stopped at some lane connecting Sinhagad road"

"We have to be quick then, speed up," I said to the driver.

"Sir, but Suraj's mobile location is still in Swargate," Inspector Bhosale interrupted me.

"No point, Bhosale. *Tithe kahi milnar nahi* (we won't get anything there). Ask the other team to reach Swargate, we can't afford to waste time."

Our car raced down the road. I was sweating from stress. Being my first day, I knew nothing about Pune and its roads. I couldn't suggest any shortcuts; all I did was depend upon Inspector Bhosale and the driver. It was one of those cases where everybody involved was filled with anxiety, nervousness, and uncertainty.

The next moment, we received a call from the other police team saying that they had found Suraj's mobile at Swargate, but there was no sign of the person who carried it. My assumption turned out to be correct. The mobile had been thrown out on the street and the murderer had headed somewhere else.

"Quite an intelligent person!" I exclaimed to myself.

Speeding down the roads, we reached the location where Ajay's mobile had been detected over the GPS. As we came to a dead end, I saw an Audi parked there. I raced towards the car but there were no signs of Ajay or anyone else.

We spotted a small house nearby, made up of bricks. It appeared as though no human activity had ever taken place there. With the overgrown grass around, the place looked like one of those haunted houses—just like the ones we see in horror movies. The bushes were unkempt with the uneven grass growing shabbily. Garbage was strewn all over the place.

As we went towards the house, I saw blood on the ground. On following its trail, we found a body. I turned it over. It was Ajay. I checked his pulse rate but it was of no use. He was already cold. We pulled on our gloves and started investigating the area. I called the unknown number and found it ringing in Ajay's pocket. It was probably Ajay's second number which we were unaware of. Ajay had been brutally killed, even worse than Rohan. His lower body was naked and a broken glass bottle was inserted into his anus. His face was bruised. Lastly, his throat had been slit to end the torture.

I felt sorry for him. I was enraged from within.

How could someone be so cruel? I thought.

After checking the body thoroughly, I called an ambulance and dispatched the body for autopsy. Although there was practically nothing more left to cut in the body, it was a murder case and rules had to be followed. The murderer was on a killing spree and I felt worried for the innocent lives put to threat.

"*Saheb, apli vat lagli ata* (Sir, we have a tough time now)," remarked Inspector Bhosale as we sat in our car.

"Why? What happened now?" I asked him in a tense voice.

"Saheb, *ha* Ajay, minister *Joshincha mulga ahe* (Sir, this Ajay is a son of minister Joshi)."

I was puzzled, lost for words. Now this piece of information was enough to ensure that we were going to have sleepless nights.

Soon, I started receiving calls from the minister's PA, higher-ranking officers, and then finally, the minister. The IG called for an urgent meeting. Later, there was a meeting with minister Joshi. Naturally, he couldn't control his emotions, yet he managed to speak and ordered us to find the culprit at the earliest.

Pressure from higher officers, the department, and politicians, coupled with some stress from within increased our workload. It was my first day in the city and I knew very little about it as I wasn't even acquainted with the change, but I kept my mind focused on the case.

16 May 2015

A new day began with a bright morning and sparkling sunshine, but for many, the brightness was not enough to overpower the darkness of their lives. They were under the blanket of gloom and waited for the ray of hope that could bring justice to innocent lives.

We had been working the whole night. Political workers dashed into the police station, ordering us to find the guilty as soon as possible. All other cases were set aside. I developed a headache, thinking about the case, working out various permutations and combinations. In all this chaos, why should the media feel left out? They didn't miss a single chance to add fuel to the already tense situation.

"Sir, what do you think? Who could be behind these serial murders?" asked one reporter.

Another asked, "What measures is the police department taking?"

A third one asked, "*Muljrim ko pakadne me aur kitna time lagega? Kya aap bata sakte hain*? (How much time do you need to catch the murderer? Can you tell us?)"

To all of them who bombarded us with questions, Inspector Bhosale and I replied in unison, "We are trying our best, the whole department is working on the case and we will find the murderer soon."

Some, not-so-generous ones, said, "*Tumhala nahi watat*, police department *aaropi la pakdayla asamarth ahe* (Don't you think the police department is incapable in catching the murderer?)."

All we did was ignore them and return to our work. I called all the staff members for a short meeting. Our department's prestige was at stake and this was tied with my will to nab the murderer. Also, I felt my rage well up inside every time I recalled the brutality with which all the three people had been killed.

"Sir, there was some court case a few months back on

the three who have been murdered," Inspector Bhosale said, adding to the information on the case. Finally, we were getting somewhere; the mystery was unleashing itself slowly.

"I want the file. Bring in all the details you can get, at the earliest," I ordered all the staff members in general.

In about fifteen minutes, Inspector Bhosale came back with the information and handed it to me. I went through the contents of the case file. I checked the name of the person who had pulled the three dead men to court. I gathered all information I could get about him.

Personal information:

Name	-	Rohit Jadhav
Age	-	25
Profession	-	Student, completed M.B.B.S. from Bharat Medical College in 2014

I made a few phone calls and found some information about the lawyer, L. Mohite, who was incharge of the case. "Track Mohite now, he is the next target," I said, getting up from my chair.

Inspector Bhosale dialled his number but the lawyer's assistant said that his boss was busy on a case. So, we decided to head towards the court house and reached there in a few minutes. We parked our car inside the court premises and waited for the ongoing session to end. After a long wait, we finally saw the lawyer heading out of the court. I stepped out of the car and began walking towards him, but suddenly, a man came running out of nowhere and stabbed the lawyer twice in his abdomen. Before we could even realise what had happened, he was done with his job.

The next minute or maybe even less than that—I didn't count—the crowd began to shout and started gathering around the body. Some started running here and there, creating chaos. The murderer began running in the opposite direction. I chased him. He passed the main entrance of the court. I followed him with Inspector Bhosale rapidly catching up with me. The fugitive ran at full pace and I kept my speed. He sprinted down the alley. I caught up with him and grabbed him by his collar, yet he continued to run. A moment later, he managed to slip from my hands.

Inspector Bhosale shouted continuously, "Stop! Stop! Stop now!"

Our driver followed us in our police jeep. The court security staff also assisted us. I continued to chase my target, and caught hold of his shirt again, jumping off from a few steps of the entrance of the park nearby. He fell to the ground and I punched him hard.

He pleaded, "Please, please let me go; I have some important work to do, please!"

Is he mentally sick? I thought, astonished. He had murdered a person just a few minutes ago and now had the audacity to plead with me to let him go claiming he had important work to do!

"What work?" I shouted, aiming another punch at his face.

"Please, sir, I'll come back again, please let me go. Trust me I will surrender," he continued to plead.

"What work?" I asked him again, raising my voice and gripping him by his collar as he tried to break free and run.

"I have to kill someone, please let me go," he said.

What a nut-case, I thought!

After solving more than sixty murder cases and being a part of solving at least hundred, this was the first time that a murderer was pleading to be allowed to run free so that he could kill someone else.

"I promise I will come back," he said and pushed me back with renewed strength.

He started running again.

"Stop!" I shouted.

(He didn't.)

"Freeze!" I shouted again.

(He didn't.)

Finally, I was left with no choice but to use my gun and taking aim, I pulled the trigger. The bullet hit him below his knee cap and he started limping. I ran towards him and held him. He attempted to run again and just kept on shouting, "Please let me go!"

I held him by his collar and dragged him to the police jeep, which had arrived by then.

24 August 2015 (The Present)

Our mouths were wide open in shocked surprise. We were overawed and terrified listening to what the officer had just narrated.

"He must be seriously mentally ill!" exclaimed Varun.

"Like how could he just expect that you'll let him go and kill someone else? I guess he has some split personality . . . what do you think, Nikhil?" he continued.

Nikhil didn't reply. He was shocked by the gruesome story and so was I.

"Sir, but why did he kill the four of them? There must be some reason, right?" I asked the officer.

"A cruel mind, that's all I can say for now," he replied.

We could sense that there was something the officer was trying to hide.

"Are you hiding something, sir?" Varun dared to ask.

"Look boys, I can't tell you anything more right now. Whatever Rohit Jadhav, the murderer, told me, I can't disclose it. It might be that he is trying to just fool me. I am not even permitted to disclose the court case, as I am yet to validate certain things. His friend Alok, who is originally from Satara and pursuing his post-graduation course in Bharat Medical College has been asked to report here. We have to confirm certain facts with him as he is Rohit's college mate and also his best-friend. That's it for now."

"Okay, sir, thank you for all the help. That was more than a shock for us," Nikhil replied, clearly terrified.

"Please keep whatever you heard to yourself for now," the officer told us.

We readily agreed in unison and then thanked him again for his time. He then casually asked us about our lifestyle, our college, and what we were pursuing, to which we responded.

As we left the police station, Nikhil asked me, "Now, what next?"

I was quiet for a while and then replied, "Let's go to Alok's college."

"And how are we supposed to know where Alok studies?" Varun asked me, absent-mindedly.

"If you remember the officer did mention Alok's college. He said Alok is doing some post-graduation course in Bharat College, remember?" I asked him.

"Oh yeah! I almost forgot that!" exclaimed Varun as he sat on his bike.

We decided to call it a day and Nikhil and I planned to find Alok the next day. Varun had some work and couldn't join us. It was going to be tough tracking Alok but we didn't want to give up. With whatever the police officer had told us, I had arrived at the assumption that Rohit did not in the least bit seem innocent. I had second thoughts about there being more to Rohit's life than what was apparent—some kind of a bad past that had turned him into a criminal. Every time I thought of him, I conjured up a villainous persona, just like the ones on TV—shabbily dressed, unshaven, long messy hair, ragged clothes, unhealed scars, and violence-filled eyes. I wondered whether his desperate want, which appeared more of a need, was perhaps not a crime; there was probably an unhealed deep wound inside him. Was he really a criminal or were the four people he killed the real villains of his story?

Finding Alok—Gathering Pieces of a Jigsaw Puzzle
25 August 2015

Early the next morning, Nikhil and I left for Alok's college. Unaware of the college timings and what course Alok was pursuing, we headed to the college office. It was around 10:00 a.m. I approached one of the clerks there and asked him about Alok. Just as we expected, he replied, "*Kon Alok? Surname batao . . . Aur hum aise kisiki jankari nahi de sakte* (Who Alok? What is his surname? And we can't disclose anyone's identity)."

Who the hell knows his surname, I thought to myself.

I asked Nikhil to go looking in another department or enquire elsewhere. I also told him to be in contact with me. We split and I headed towards the college canteen and struck up a conversation with some students who seemed like post-grads. I observed the people passing by and looked at the name tags pinned to their white aprons.

I had explored the college and the hospital but found it almost impossible to trace Alok. While passing through one of the corridors, I spotted 'Alok' written on one of the student's name tags. I stopped him immediately and started talking to him and our conversation went something like this:

"Yes, I am Alok."

"Yes, I am pursuing a post-graduation course over here."

"Rohit? . . . Yeah, I know him . . . he must be in the canteen."

"Canteen?" I asked, a little confused by his answer.

And to my utter disappointment, I realised he was talking about someone named Rohit Mehta and not Rohit Jadhav.

"Did you find him?" Nikhil asked me when we met in the parking area, about an hour later.

"No," I replied, with my hands in my pockets and kicking the pebbles on the uneven parking ground. I was more irritated than upset.

It seemed almost impossible to find the right Alok. We finally decided to give up for the day and headed to our bikes. Often, when there is no hope and no way out, certainly that's where luck plays its role. Somewhere, a miracle takes place and that's what happened next. We had been searching for Alok and the very moment we gave up, I saw an MH-11 white Alto car entering the parking area.

MH-11—that's Satara! said the lightbulb that went on in my head. ACP Deshmukh had mentioned Alok's hometown.

We quickly advanced towards the person and when we approached him, we saw 'Alok' written on his badge. Somewhere, hope rose in my heart. We reached the person and I began asking him his name and if he knew someone named Rohit. Initially, he tried to avoid us but when we disclosed our identity and what we were up to, he relaxed and seemed ready to help. I couldn't help thinking that destiny had brought him to us.

"I want to write about Rohit's life. I think there is something more to him than what the media and the police are telling us. Can you please help us?" I requested Alok.

"Uh . . . it's a little difficult. You know, he is in police custody and it is kind of difficult for everyone," replied Alok, probably afraid that he may be accused of something that was best left alone.

We tried to convince him, but he smartly evaded our request with excuses.

"Isn't he your friend? Can't you do this for him?" Nikhil questioned Alok.

Alok remained silent for a while. He seemed to be reconsidering but was probably confused or maybe even disturbed by the question.

"Please," I tried cajoling him.

He remained quiet and then replied, "Only for him, I can try. I hope I can trust you."

"Yeah, we promise that we won't get you into any trouble. I only want to write about his life, and that too, with your consent," I replied, happy that we had succeeded in convincing him.

We decided on the venue and time. Alok was quite busy and as I, too, had to attend college in the morning, we chose to meet at around 6:00 p.m. the next day at Alok's place. He had rented a flat in Pune and gave us the address.

26 August 2015 – Alok's House

Nikhil and I reached Alok's house at 6:00 p.m. sharp. He offered us a seat. I glanced around his flat. In spite of living alone, I found the rooms neat and tidy. It was nothing like a college student's flat—shabby, cluttered, or in a state of mayhem.

Alok was about five feet and eight inches tall, with a dusky complexion and straight hair. He wore spectacles that suited him.

He offered us water and brought in some snacks, which he had probably ordered in anticipation of our visit.

"Make yourselves comfortable. Please feel at home," he said with a smile.

We smiled back and thanked him. We chatted for a while about general things. Alok mentioned Rohit often in the conversation, indicating that they might have been the best of friends. After about half an hour, we requested Alok to tell us about Rohit's life. I had my pen and notebook ready to take notes.

Taking a deep breath, Alok began . . .

CHAPTER 2

We Had to Be Friends!

It was July 2009 when I got admission into Bharat Medical College. For as long as I can remember, I had dreamt of pursuing medicine and my wish had come true. I lived in Satara and appeared for my board exams there and had managed to score good marks in the CET examination, at least enough to secure admission into this college. Somewhere in mid-July was my first day of college. With my parent's blessings, I stepped into the college. Lectures were due to begin in a couple of days. All we were told by the authorities was to settle down first.

As I entered the main gate, I was awestruck by the infrastructure. It left me spellbound. It was a private college and my parents had strived hard to earn every last note of the yearly fees to be paid. I thanked them over the phone. There was quite a lot of greenery around. The college was clean and well-maintained. I wore my backpack, just like school children do, and explored the campus. I looked for my hostel and soon found it. My room was on the fourth floor. I entered my room and kept my luggage. As I looked around the small room, I knew I was going to miss my home. I saw that there were already a number of bags and I assumed they were my room partner's. Having nothing to do, I sat and waited for him.

After almost an hour, I heard someone say, "Hello . . . this is Rohit." I looked around and found a guy standing in front of me, hand outstretched.

"Hello," I replied, shaking his hand.

"No need to introduce yourself, you're Alok from Satara, right? I checked your name from the hostel list and then found out about you," he said, interrupting me. He then smiled and sprang upon the bed.

Rohit seemed like a stud, that's what I could figure out right away. He had a muscular body, straight hair, fair complexion, perfect—just like a model. He was taller than me, in fact much taller—about six feet with long legs that added to his personality.

"Look, everything mine is yours, just don't be fussy and try to co-operate with my nonsense," he said, winking at me.

I didn't understand what he meant by terms like 'fussy', 'nonsense', and 'co-operating', but still nodded in agreement. He asked me a whole lot of questions. We tried to get friendlier with each other. To me, Rohit seemed like a good guy at the moment; yet I tried to be cautious as my family always bombarded me with stories of various mishaps that happen in college life—including drug abuse and ragging.

I was new to Pune but Rohit was a local. He knew almost every small place in the city. I took it in a positive way as it would help me get acquainted with my new home. Rohit was staying with me in the hostel since his house was almost an hour away from our college. Also, his parents didn't want him to waste time in travelling. I guess Rohit didn't give a damn about time. He was here to enjoy life—at least that's what his attitude suggested.

***

"Dude, get up, we are late, we have to go to college," I shouted in Rohit's ear and almost kicked him off the bed.

It was our first day and I was excited. I sincerely packed all my books into my bag—after all it was the beginning of the course. Rohit brushed his teeth and went for a quick bath. He tried on various T-shirts, finding it difficult to choose one.

"What are you doing? Hurry up and wear something fast!" I exclaimed.

"Yeah, just a minute, it's the first day and you know I want to create a good impression," replied Rohit with a wink, finally deciding to wear a blue T-shirt. He then added, "I hope you understand what I mean to say."

"I don't want to be late on the first day," I continued.

"*Kuch nahi hota, dude* . . . chill!" retorted Rohit and then started combing his hair.

"And as if you are going to pay attention to the lecture on the very first day! I'd rather be checking out some of the hot chicks over here," he continued and winked at me.

He sprayed on some deodorant and then we left together.

"So, you're not interested in girls?" Rohit asked me as we passed the canteen.

"No, never thought of it. Let's see what comes up here," I replied.

"Did you have a girlfriend in the past?"

"Not that lucky!" I said with laughter, "What about you?"

"Had one, but things didn't work out and we broke up."

"Oh, I am sorry."

"Don't be, I am not! It's kind of common these days. Who cares! I tell you there is no love, all you see is infatuation."

I smiled with no first-hand experience of what he was saying. We went into the auditorium, where the Principal was supposed to address us. With almost 150 students, the auditorium seemed to be full. We were late and found seats in the last row.

"We should have come a bit earlier," I said, taking a seat.

"It is better here, you get a good view of what has to be viewed," he whispered with a naughty smile.

"Good morning, students, and welcome to our prestigious college. I congratulate you on behalf of our college authorities . . ." the principal began.

Rohit switched on his music player and plugged in his headphones. He was least interested in what was going on. I chose to show some respect to the principal and whatever he had to say.

"Look there, 12 o'clock, she is so hot!" whispered Rohit, all of a sudden.

"And 2 o'clock, the green dress, she definitely is the best. I guess 32-28-36 . . . too sexy," he continued.

"Shhh . . . stop it!" I remarked, with a finger on my lips.

"It's making me crazy! Good time to be spent here," Rohit was in no mood to stop.

From the stage, the principal continued, "There are many distractions that may cross your way. An ideal student is the one who conquers those and walks on the right track. Remember, students, medicine is not an easy course."

"As if he didn't enjoy his college life! *Pakau, bas kar*!" said Rohit.

The principal probably repeated the same speech every year. It was boring and I, too, began to look around. I chatted with the guy sitting next to me. On the other side was Rohit, who seemed to be busy with his so-called 'good scenery.'

"Dude . . . look there! three rows ahead of us . . . left side, black T-shirt . . . she looks good!" I said this time and pointed towards the girl.

"*Oyye teri*! She is superb!" he exclaimed. "So you are picking up fast ha!" he teased me.

I smiled looking at him.

"Bad luck, friend, *ye teri bhabhi hai*!" he continued.

"Huh?" I exclaimed.

"Dude, she is just too good. I am going to try my luck with her. I think it will go well!"

It is pretty fascinating and probably happens only in India where a girl becomes your friend's 'bhabhi' before she becomes your 'girlfriend' or 'wife'.

I smiled at my own thought.

"So, all the best," I wished Rohit, after a pause.

The principal still continued with his lecture and my friend continued to stare at the girl I had pointed at.

"What if she has a boyfriend?" I asked Rohit.

"Listen, even if there is a goal keeper defending the goal post, no matter what, the players succeed in scoring a goal. Same thing applies here! And say, if she refuses, then I'll find a new goal post," he replied, winking at me.

I laughed at his thought. Certainly, it told me that Rohit was practical in life. He had that 'X-factor' in him that made me feel he was cool. Oh, wait a minute, I am not gay!

***

"Let's sit here!" Rohit pointed towards a bench as the lecture began, after the principal's address. We had three subjects for the year—Anatomy, Physiology, and Biochemistry, which were as vast as the ocean. Added to the principal's warning, the size of the books was fuel to the fire and frightened me. I paid attention to what was going on in class but Rohit had his eyes somewhere else. It was then that I noticed that the girl sitting ahead of us was the same girl we had seen in the auditorium.

"Hi, my name's Rohit," Rohit introduced himself to her when she randomly checked the strength of the class by turning around.

"Hiee, I am Aisha," she introduced herself and went through a formal handshake.

She was indeed beautiful with fair skin, blue eyes, and even teeth. She was shorter than Rohit, who seemed to be about six feet tall. *She's probably 5'10"*, I thought.

She was sitting alone. Rohit wanted to sit next to her but felt it was inappropriate to leave me and go. I could sense it through his body language.

"Hey, I can't see properly from here. I'll better go and sit on one of the front benches, is it fine with you?" I asked Rohit.

"Well, no problem, as you wish, bro," he replied smiling, his expression obviously thankful.

I went ahead and so did Rohit, to sit next to Aisha, after seeking her permission.

"So, where are you from?" Rohit asked her.

"New Delhi—a long way away and missing my place," she replied, smiling.

"Pune isn't that bad!"

"No, I didn't mean that. I mean missing my family," she interrupted Rohit, taking down notes from the blackboard.

"Oh! Well, I am from Pune. It is a really good place. Forget the place, the people are really lovable. Spend time with them and you will understand," Rohit winked at her.

"Ha ha ha! Let's see, time will tell how people are," she replied with some laughter.

"Now please let us pay attention. It's our first day; let us not create a bad impression. Sir has been continuously keeping a watch on us," she said while drawing the diagrams of leucocytes from the PowerPoint presentation.

Rohit had no choice but to listen to her. He kept looking at her from the corner of his eye. She was writing down whatever sir said and Rohit was the complete opposite, just wasting time.

***

"Hiee, what's up?" Aisha sent him a text message.

"I am fine, just unpacking my bag," replied Rohit.

"What about you?" he asked her.

"Bored with the new place, feel like running away."

"Don't think of anything like that, a new place may be boring but a new friend like me might not be," he went on flirtatiously.

"Ha ha ha . . . But when the hell did we become friends? :p"

"I guess today, didn't we?"

"Probably, I don't know! Well I just forgot to call my mom today, she is gonna kill me. Talk to you later, bye."

"Alright, give my regards to your mom and yeah do tell her how your new friend is, *chal* bye, cya!"

"Ha ha ha . . . okay, bye!"

***

It did start formally, but as days passed both Rohit and Aisha became informal and comfortable with each other. They shared a good rapport. I was also introduced to Aisha, who introduced her roommate, Neha, to us.

"You are going a bit too fast," I said to Rohit, one day in the hostel room.

"Fast! You must be insane," he replied instantly. "I haven't even called her on a date," he added.

I had no answer to that, preferring to be silent. Getting a bit serious he went on, "Shall I invite her on a date?"

"Are you crazy? It is too early," I replied in a hurry.

He was compelled to get back into his thinking mode. After a while he came up with an idea. "Let's invite her for a cup of coffee or snacks, what say?" he asked me.

"What if she rejects?"

"Man! Say something positive at least once in a while," he looked upset.

"I mean it will look odd if you go alone with her or invite her with just the two of us," I remarked.

"What do you mean?"

"I mean she will feel uncomfortable to be the only girl along with us boys. You need to invite Neha as well," I said.

"Alright," that's all he said and switched off the light.

It did feel strange for me but I let go of the situation and dozed off to sleep.

The next day, we went to college as usual and attended the lectures and the practical classes. During dissection, Rohit walked to Neha and said something to her. I was scared. I knew he was inviting Aisha and her to some place. The fear of rejection gripped me. Later, they were joined by Aisha and the three of them discussed something. I had no idea what they were talking about.

"What happened?" I asked him as he returned to our dissection table.

"They are coming to CCD after the dissections," he replied, delightedly.

"What? Don't tell me! Are you serious? How did you convince them?" I asked, incredulously.

He laughed and then looking at me replied, "I said that you had a break-up and so I am giving you a break-up party. I asked them to join in and cheer you up."

"What the hell? Are you fucking crazy?" I hit him hard on his head.

"It hurts, idiot." he shouted in retaliation.

"You have to be low and sad all the time, just act as if you are miserable over your break-up," he teased me and received another blow on his head.

I just couldn't get it. What was he up to? I was probably the only guy in the world who had a break-up without even having a girlfriend ever in my life. I had to act sad—but having been single all my life, I hardly knew how it felt to go through a break-up.

"I am not doing this," I said to him.

"*Bhai hai na tu mera?* Marriot *mein* party (Bro, I'll give you a party in Marriot)."

Now who the hell declines such a party offer? I did accept it at the end, after making a lot of fuss and pretending his party didn't really matter to me.

As decided, after the dissection, Rohit and I headed towards CCD. The girls were going to join us later. All of a sudden it started raining.

"Oh fuck! Why the hell did it have to rain today?" shouted Rohit in frustration.

"They won't come, leave it," I said as we both took shelter in a shed.

"Shut up!" he hit me on my head. "Let's go," he further added.

"What? It's raining!"

"You are not going to die!" he made a face and pulled me along.

In spite of the heavy rain, we ran towards our hostel.

"I am going to kill you," I shouted as we kept running.

"Just run!" he replied as we ran. We were wet from head to toe and the water seeping inside our jeans made it difficult to run.

In no time we reached our hostel. We ran up the stairs to our room. Rohit opened the door and immediately headed to his wardrobe.

"Change your clothes fast," he said, and wiping off his body with a towel quickly wore a white T-shirt and black pants. I had to keep pace with him.

"Let's go," he said again, and grabbing an umbrella, we reached CCD. "Will they come?" Rohit asked me.

"I told you they won't come. It's raining heavily," I replied back.

"Fuck off!" he saluted me with the middle finger. "Be positive sometimes," he went on.

I hid my laughter as I sat on one of the chairs. While I glanced at the menu card, Rohit walked to the door, peeped outside, looked for signs of Aisha, then checked his mobile to see if there was network, checked my mobile and then walked towards me and asked me again if they would come. Without waiting for my response, he repeated the same process.

After a while, he saw Aisha and Neha on the street. As they crossed the road, Rohit came running towards me.

"They have come!" he said, all excited.

"Shhhh," he placed a finger on his lips and continued, "Act depressed, you've had a break-up." He then walked towards the girls and greeted them.

Soon, everyone was comfortably seated and the conversation began.

"Why did you break up with your girlfriend, Alok?" Aisha asked the most difficult question we had expected but weren't prepared with an answer.

"Ugh," I kept thinking. Rohit looked at me and immediately whispered into Aisha's ears, "It's better we don't discuss it now, he is very upset, I hope you can understand."

"It happens, Alok! You will find a better girl, don't

worry, dear," she tried motivating me and I maintained a sunken face. Soon, Neha joined her and together, they continued to console me and this actually embarrassed me even more.

Once our snacks were on the table, we began to enjoy it. The topic soon shifted from my break-up to the dos and don'ts in a relationship. Rohit, Aisha, and Neha went ahead with the conversation while I abused Rohit in my mind. I felt awkward that I had become the topic of conversation.

The evening soon ended and we headed back to our respective hostels. On our way, I continued to abuse Rohit and he laughed over my sad state. All in all, the day had definitely been a memorable one for both of us—one that we could pen down somewhere and laugh over years later.

***

College life seemed to be fun for all of us. We were enjoying each and every moment we spent together. Rohit always sat beside Aisha during the lectures and she didn't mind. On top of it, both of them were in the same batch for practicals, which gave Rohit additional time to spend with her.

"Hey, what are you doing?" Rohit asked Aisha, calling her one day at about seven in the evening.

"Nothing, just completing my Haematology journal," she said.

"I am pretty bored, let's go and have some coffee, what do you say?" suggested Rohit.

"Hmm . . ."

"What's there to think? *Chal*, let's go."

"And what about the journal?" she asked.

"I'll help you with it later, c'mon get up," insisted Rohit.

"Hmm . . . okay fine! I'll meet you in ten minutes. I'll get ready, bye," she said and hung up.

Rohit smiled at me. He probably meant 'one more step ahead'. This time it was only the two of them. He went to the bathroom and got ready in the next ten minutes. He applied gel to his hair and left the room. He walked towards the girls' hostel. On his way, he kept fidgeting with his shirt and checking his hair with his hand while he removed his mobile so that he could see himself on the screen and double check if everything was okay.

"You're late!" exclaimed Aisha, when Rohit met her outside her hostel.

"Sorry, I thought girls take more time to get ready, so thought of giving you some extra time," replied Rohit, laughing.

"Not always actually! Chuck it! Where are we going?" asked Aisha.

"Coffee house or Burger Point?"

"I guess both, I am quite hungry," replied Aisha, grinning. Rohit agreed and they both set off.

The weather was good. It was evening and a little breezy, causing Aisha's hair to fly. As they walked, they continuously chatted with each other. In no time they both were outside the college campus.

"You are looking pretty," Rohit appreciated Aisha's dressing sense, glancing at her attire and immediately looked down when their eyes met.

She had worn a red V-neck top and dark blue jeans.

"Thank you, by the way I always look good!" she boasted, which made both of them laugh.

They first went to Burger Point as Aisha insisted. She ordered a chicken burger while Rohit went with a vegetarian one.

"It's pretty tasty," said Aisha, biting into the burger.

"So, are you acquainted with Pune life?" Rohit asked her in a childish tone.

"Yeah, but I still miss Delhi, my parents, and all my relatives," replied Aisha, making a fussy face.

"They aren't coming here to meet you? I mean your parents."

"Dad's a doctor, a gynaecologist, so it becomes difficult for him to spare time from his busy schedule and the emergency cases he has in the hospital, but my mom can come and I think she might probably be visiting me next week."

"Oh! That's great! Do you miss anyone else?" asked Rohit, wiping his mouth.

"Who anyone else?" asked Aisha in a puzzled tone.

"Boyfriend? Long distance?"

"Ahh no, I did have one but then we broke up in two months, things kind of didn't go well between us."

Rohit was happy listening to her talk. But he kept the happiness to himself and didn't let it show on his face. He secretly danced and grooved inside.

"What about you?" asked Aisha, munching on her burger.

"No, no girlfriends," replied Rohit.

"Strange!" exclaimed Aisha.

"Like, you are handsome, I mean anyone might fall for you," she continued.

"Even you?" winked Rohit.

"Ahh, maybe!" replied Aisha, blushing.

Rohit smiled. He knew he was on the right path. He hoped for something positive in the near future.

"*Jyada soch mat*! Let's go!" continued Aisha, laughing, and grabbed his hand to take him to the coffee house.

Her touch set off sensations inside Rohit, as if the moment had frozen and everything around him moved in slow motion. Her soft hands were like cushions stuffed with silk cotton. He was speechless for a while. He was holding Aisha's hand for the very first time and this sent butterflies fluttering in his stomach.

***

"She's amazing, dude," Rohit told me for almost the tenth time since he had returned.

"Her hand is so soft, she is the one, Alok! She is the one I was waiting for!" he continued.

"Does she have a boyfriend?" I asked him, setting aside

the anatomy text book I had been reading since the last one hour.

"She had, but now she is single."

"Did you tell her about your past?" I asked him.

"I said I had no girlfriend, I lied."

"Bro! Was there any need to lie?"

"How the hell will she come to know? I had two, each lasted for a month, and they weren't actually relationships!" he replied, again texting Aisha.

"But what if she finds it out in the future?"

"She won't! Chill!" replied Rohit, in a carefree voice.

***

Four months had passed since our college began and Rohit-Aisha became good friends. Their friendship bloomed with each passing day. Rohit, Aisha, Neha, and I would often hang out at different places. Movies and dinner, and wherever we went, Aisha would always sit next to Rohit. On top of it, Neha would stay back with me to give Aisha some quality time with Rohit. It seemed like there was some response from Aisha's end as well. It appeared as if they were both made for each other.

One odd day, we finally had our fresher's party—an unofficial one. We had been waiting for it and at last the day was here.

"Let's go together, what do you say?" Aisha asked Rohit, calling him on his mobile.

Rohit was hardly going to refuse. So, Neha and I, along

with two other college friends had to hire a cab, while Rohit was all set to let his Kawasaki-Ninja go top speed. We had to reach Pesto Pesto – a famous lounge in Pune at around 8:00 p.m. As it was an unofficial party given by the seniors, we couldn't disclose anything to the college teachers and staff. Rohit and I bribed our hostel watchman, while Aisha and Neha requested their watchman. Aisha was against bribing, so found a good way out. We would return by 12 or 1 at night, so turning the watchman into an ally was quite necessary for all of us.

As decided, I waited with Neha and two others for our cab while Rohit and Aisha walked towards the bike. Rohit wore a black leather jacket, denim jeans, and night glasses which made him look perfect to woo the girls. He had a French beard, which made him look sexy. His Ninja was just the cherry on the cake.

Some other college students looked at him, as if implying he was a show-off but it hardly bothered him. Aisha looked marvellous. She was wearing a red thigh-length party dress. Her lips shone with red gloss and she wore her hair loose. Rohit couldn't help expressing his feelings, "Wow! You look hot!" His mouth was wide open. Aisha blushed, and then burst out laughing when she saw his expression.

"C'mon let's get going," said Neha, exasperated with the never-ending complimenting session going on between the two of them. We left together, leaving the two behind.

Aisha sat on Rohit's bike, holding his shoulder for support.

"*Chale*, madam?" asked Rohit, turning on his bike.

"Yeah, let's go!" shouted Aisha in excitement.

Rohit set off at a good speed. Aisha held on to him. Her untied hair waved with the breeze. She looked bold and beautiful while Rohit stole the show with his physique.

We reached on time and waited for the two to arrive. They appeared a while later; probably Rohit had purposely taken a longer route.

"He really rides well," Aisha complimented Rohit as she met Neha.

"*Bas na*! He is not a film star," Neha pulled Aisha's leg.

I couldn't stop laughing and all Rohit could say in embarrassment was, "I'll park my bike and get back."

Aisha elbowed Neha hard enough to make her shout in pain. Aisha kept a grumpy face. We went ahead and collected our passes from the seniors. It was a couple pass and it was obvious that 'Rohit-Aisha' would choose to go together and 'Neha and I' would go together as we were the only ones left behind.

"Dude! She is so hot," whispered Rohit, pointing towards the senior who was distributing the entry passes and exposing a bit too much in her low-necked dress.

"Rohit, shame on you! You should have your eyes on someone else," I replied. I think I was a bit too loud.

"What happened?" questioned Aisha on hearing me and watching Rohit smile at my response.

"Nothing," I replied to Aisha.

We went inside. It was the first time I had entered into a lounge for there were none in Satara. It looked like fun to me.

There was a dance floor and the DJ tuned in to some rocking foot-tapping music. Soon, everyone started moving to the beat. All our colleagues looked quite different in the disco lights. Aisha pulled Rohit to the dance floor. She changed her gears to top speed as her favourite song 'Desi girl' began. The song was amongst the top ten songs that year—2009.

"Why are you so uncomfortable?" Aisha asked Rohit, as loud as she could to get herself heard over the music.

"Wait a minute," replied Rohit and went to have some shots of vodka.

"You drink?" Aisha asked him.

"Yeah, don't you?"

"No, I hate it."

I had never tried booze and so I didn't know what really makes people go crazy after having some, but I was not against it and wouldn't mind trying it sometime. The drinks made Rohit more confident and he could easily dance to every song that was being played. He brought a Budweiser next.

Rohit insisted that Aisha should have a sip out of his bottle. She denied at the start but later ended up having a couple of sips even though she didn't quite like it.

"Yuck it's too bad!" she exclaimed, making a face.

"It happens the first time," replied Rohit and both resumed dancing to the music being played.

Aisha looked very beautiful as she jumped and moved her body to the beat of the song. Rohit gazed at her and was lost in her eyes. Aisha looked into his eyes. Both kept staring at each other for a while. As the music turned romantic,

Rohit held her hand and pulled her close to him. With his other hand on her waist, he made her move to the music. Aisha seemed to be frightened but soon she, too, gave in. I could find love for Rohit in her eyes. She seemed to be attracted towards him. I wished they'd both admit it to each other soon. Throughout the party neither Rohit nor Aisha left each other's company.

"Chalo, let's go!" said Neha and that's when both of them realised it was already past midnight.

We came out of the club. Rohit was still high. He was out of control but still managed to walk. His eyes said it all, that he was no way in his senses.

"It was fun!" Aisha said excitedly, almost jumping over Rohit. He managed to smile. I knew he had consumed too much alcohol.

"Rohit, you and Aisha take a cab; I'll go with Neha on the bike. I think you won't be able to ride," I said turning towards him.

"Ahh no, I can," he replied with his heavy tongue.

"No, let's take a cab," Aisha interrupted us.

Probably she thought of Rohit's safety. Rohit was not going to object to her and he immediately agreed.

Soon, both got into the cab we had called and I walked along with Neha towards the bike.

"It was fun *na*?" Aisha asked Rohit for the second time as they settled in and the cab started moving.

"Yeah and you looked pretty good today," said Rohit, closing his eyes and resting his head back. Aisha imitated him and found it to be funny.

Both chatted with their eyes closed. Rohit had a reason as he was drunk but Aisha didn't seem to have a reason. After all girls will be girls! They like silly things and carry them out with perfection. The silliest things look cute to them and so did this one.

"Don't you think you drank too much?" Aisha continued.

"Actually, I am addicted to it, can't leave it now. And you know, it feels better after you have some," replied Rohit in a heavy voice.

"I'll help you. Please leave it, there's nothing good about it."

"And what about you? Didn't you drink today?"

"I did but that was for the first time. I have control and I would never have it on a daily basis. I don't mind if someone drinks once in a blue moon."

"So that 'someone' is me?"

"Yeah."

"Why me?"

Aisha remained quiet for a while and then replied, "Because, I care about you!"

She paused, and then continued, "I can promise you that I won't touch alcohol in my life."

"Really? You will never touch it?" asked Rohit, opening his eyes.

"Challenge me," replied Aisha with her notorious smile.

"But I can't!" said Rohit, again resting his head on the seat.

"I said na, I'll help you—just co-operate with me, there is nothing impossible in life."

"Let's see," replied Rohit, closing his eyes and was almost half asleep.

His body ached as he had danced a lot. Looking at Rohit, Aisha too closed her eyes. She soon felt asleep. She rested her head on Rohit's shoulder and this woke him up. He looked at her. She looked cuter when she was asleep. He tucked her hair behind her ear as it was constantly falling over her face. He stroked her head with his hand. His attraction for her was growing. It was probably taking its next step towards 'love.'

In few minutes they reached the college. Rohit woke Aisha, unable to take his eyes off her beautiful face.

"We've reached," he said.

Both got out of the cab. Rohit paid the driver and they moved towards the hostel. As they came close to the girls' hostel, Aisha wished him goodnight but Rohit stopped her, catching her hand.

"What?" she asked in a drowsy voice.

He remained silent.

"What?" she asked him again.

"I . . . I love you," he stammered, but managed to look into her eyes.

She looked back into his eyes but didn't say anything. She was shocked as well as frightened of what he would do next as it was all happening late at night.

"I love you, Aisha," Rohit repeated, this time with some confidence.

"We're friends and we better remain friends," replied Aisha and let go of his hand. She turned towards the gate and entered the hostel without saying another word. She was confused as well as shocked. She thought it best to leave and that is just what she did then.

Rohit remained silent and stood rooted to the spot for a long time. He watched her leave. He was confused by what she had said. He thought she had feelings for him and so had dared to express his love for her.

He felt a slight pain as it seemed as though she had refused his proposal. 'We're friends and we better remain friends' echoed for quite some time deep inside him. Disheartened, he made his way to our hostel.

Were they meant to be friends only?

***

26 August 2015. Alok's House – The Present

"What? How could she say that?" Nikhil exclaimed, getting up from the couch.

"Yes, she did say that," said Alok, offering us coffee and some snacks.

I asked, "I thought she too had some feelings for Rohit, didn't she?"

"Even Rohit and I thought the same," replied Alok.

"So, you mean she never felt any attraction towards Rohit? What happened next?" I continued with my questions, getting a little hyper.

"Guys, chill!" exclaimed Alok.

He got up and went towards the phone on the table.

"Should I order something? What would you guys like to eat?" he continued.

"Oh please! Forget eating and first clear things for us. I'll die from suspense." Nikhil couldn't control himself.

Alok smiled and got back to us. "Okay, so Rohit came back that day . . ."

As Alok was about to continue, the bell rang and Alok went to open the door. It was Varun.

"Guys, I too want to be a part of this story," he said as he saw Nikhil and me sitting on the sofa.

We introduced Alok and Varun. We then had to brief Varun about Rohit and Aisha's story. Judging by his facial expression, we could sense his keen interest.

"Alok, please continue," said Nikhil for the second time as he was curious to know what had happened next.

Alok took a sip of water and continued, "That day, Rohit returned to our room, looking disappointed. I asked him what had happened but he was not interested in talking. He just went to sleep. The next day, as we were having breakfast, he told me everything. I too was puzzled. I advised him to give Aisha some time to think and he agreed. Throughout the day, whenever Aisha and Rohit met, he was hesitant, but Aisha was normal. Rohit seemed to act and walk differently. Everything had changed for him."

"You mean she pretended to be friendly?" asked Varun, leaning on the sofa.

"Actually, she didn't pretend. It came out naturally, as if she had forgotten that Rohit had proposed to her," replied Alok.

"And then, didn't Rohit dare to propose to her again?" I asked him.

"He did hesitate initially but after a couple of days he asked her about her feelings for him. And guess what? All she said was that Rohit was faking it and he never loved her. He wasn't serious enough, that's what she thought."

"Was she out of her senses? How could she know if he was serious or not, in just a single day?" Nikhil got up, unable to sit peacefully.

"What she meant by it was that Rohit was drunk on the day he had proposed to her and so she thought that whatever he had said wasn't him but the alcohol that had done all the talking. So, she didn't want to accept his proposal. Rohit tried his best to explain that it wasn't the alcohol that spoke!"

Varun kept staring at Alok. We all kept mum for a while and then Varun broke the silence, "Did she finally agree?"

"She did, but it took almost a fortnight. Aisha did like him from the start but had been hiding it for some unknown reason. Probably, she was testing Rohit's love for her and wanted to be convinced that he was really committed to the relationship. Rohit on the other hand tried to be as normal as he could, just being himself.

"Finally, one day she herself approached Rohit and expressed her feelings for him."

"Didn't Rohit and you think it was rather sudden?" I asked Alok, munching on a couple of chips.

"Not really, because she kept saying that she had misinterpreted Rohit's proposal as something he had done in a drunken state. Rohit found it to be a genuine reason and so did I."

"So, the love story begins!" exclaimed Nikhil, with joy.

"Yes, it does!" Alok replied but didn't seem to be happy about it.

That made the three of us quite anxious.

CHAPTER 3

Love Is Life

"Where are we going?" asked Aisha, as she sat behind Rohit on his bike.

"Just sit!" ordered Rohit with love.

"We have to get back in time. You know my warden, she is . . ."

"Shhh! How many questions are you going to ask? We are going out for dinner and don't worry, we will be back in time."

It was almost 7.00 p.m. Aisha always feared the hostel deadline. I accompanied them to the college's main gate just to bid them goodbye. It was their first date together since they were in a relationship and Rohit was trying his best to make it memorable for the two of them. Aisha had worn a blue top and dark blue denim shorts. She looked her best. Even I fell for her that day. Had she not been my friend's girlfriend, the relationship I shared with her would have probably been different.

Holding Rohit by his waist, Aisha sat behind him. Rohit drove his bike to Melange, the destination he had planned.

It was a hotel in Aundh, especially for couples who wanted some privacy and good ambience. The hotel had a terrace view from where almost half of the city could be seen. The city lights and the cool breeze made it a romantic place. There was a swimming pool at one end, and a bar counter at the other. There was music, with romantic tracks in English and Hindi. Rohit had already pre-booked a table beside the pool. The railing of the terrace was close by and both Aisha and Rohit had a panoramic view of the city from where they were seated. Red roses were arranged on the table and a candle was lit to add to the romance, which had just begun to bloom.

"Aww . . . candlelight dinner!" Aisha smiled and looked into Rohit's eyes. Her eyes sparkled with joy. "How romantic!"

As they took their places at the table, a bottle of champagne was served. All these arrangements had been made by Rohit in advance. The hotel authorities were following Rohit's instructions in the best manner possible.

"Cheers!" both shouted in unison as they clinked their glasses of champagne.

When the food was served, Aisha found a piece of paper under her plate. She opened it and read it aloud.

> **"There's so much I wanna say,
> Through words I tried to convey,
> Bombastic words and colourful phrases,
> I tried to use, but all in vain, Poems, lyrics, compositions too, I tried to write all that I feel.
> But nothing beats these simple three words:
> I love you!"**

She held Rohit's hand and said, "I love you too, Rohit!"

Rohit immediately went down on his knees with red roses in one hand and her hand in the other. He said, "I love you so much! My love will create such an impact on you that even after me, anyone in your life will have to know me first in order to know you and love you."

"Why are you thinking of leaving me? I won't and neither should you!" she replied instantly.

"I won't leave you. I love you, Aisha," Rohit replied back. He kissed her hand and continued, laughing, "I can't ask you, "will you be my Valentine?" because you already are!"

She joined in his laughter.

He then gave her a red box and asked her to open it. She curiously fidgeted with the box and then finally opened it, after asking him several times what was inside it.

Looking at the silver necklace inside, she was on cloud nine. She immediately got up and hugged Rohit.

"Thank you! It's really lovely," she said and kissed his cheeks.

Rohit asked her to turn around. Lifting her hair off her

neck, he helped her wear the necklace, hooking it behind her neck. He kissed her neck making her moan with pleasure. Aisha looked into Rohit's eyes and blushed. It sent shivers down her spine.

They both ordered the food and started eating. Rohit fed Aisha and she fed him back, getting their relationship off to a happy start.

After their dinner both headed towards the bike.

"Oh, it's late! It's already nine! Now we won't be able to get back in time," exclaimed Aisha anxiously, as she walked with Rohit, holding his hand.

"Oh shit!" exclaimed Rohit, in a panicky voice.

"Can you manage something, like ask your friend to sign against your name when the warden comes?" he continued.

"Well, that can be managed, but still I won't get an entry, the watchman won't allow me in," she replied, when they got on the bike.

"We can bribe him," Rohit suggested.

"No, no! I hate bribing," she replied, clutching his shoulders.

"Okay, alright! But at least call Neha or someone else and ask her to sign against your name," he said, as they took to the main road.

"I'll think of a way in the meantime," he continued.

Aisha called Neha and Rohit called me at the same moment to let us know they won't be able to return in time.

"Did you think of a way out?" asked Aisha, after her call ended.

"How about a Pune *darshan*? Let's roam around

everywhere, spend the whole night all by ourselves, how does that sound?" asked Rohit, hopefully.

"Are you crazy!" she shouted. "No way. It's a stupid idea," she went on.

"It will be fun, let's do it, c'mon please!" said Rohit, excited.

Aisha hesitated, but she gave in as she too found it exciting. I received a call from Rohit and I was as apprehensive as Aisha. In the end, I agreed to whatever he said.

Rohit drove his bike, while Aisha held him and rested her head on his shoulder. With no destination fixed and no plans in their mind, both roamed around aimlessly. The night was theirs and they decided to go for a movie. They found a good romantic one and after purchasing the tickets, they settled down in their seats.

As the movie commenced, Aisha held Rohit's hand and rested her head on his shoulder. He stroked her hair lovingly, while she kissed his hand and cheeks. They shared some popcorn and commented on almost every scene in the movie. The movie was boring and the script sucked. The star cast had no star power and not surprisingly, the theatre was almost empty.

Once the movie ended, both headed out blindly with no destination. It was almost 2.00 a.m. and the weather was chilly. Both shivered when Rohit's bike speeded up.

"I need a coffee or tea, it's very cold," said Aisha, grabbing Rohit by his waist. "On top of it, I have worn shorts, which makes my legs numb because of this freaking cold," she continued.

Rohit laughed when he glanced at her. Aisha punched him from behind shouting, "Stop laughing! Your idea is just too stupid! Spending the night outside in this cold weather! I shouldn't have listened to you."

She kept punching him hard from behind with her small fists. Rohit was a strong muscular guy and Aisha's punches had no impact on him.

"Ahh!" she shouted in pain.

"Okay . . . okay, let's find a coffee somewhere, but I think it may be tough to get one," replied Rohit, after a long pause.

They both searched for a coffee or a tea shop but didn't find any and so landed up at Z-bridge an hour later.

"You idiot, it's so cold!" remarked Aisha, when Rohit parked his bike and both sat on Z-bridge.

"Sorry, Aisha, but don't you find it nice to be together for a night?" Rohit asked and winked at her with a naughty smile.

"Nice my foot!" exclaimed Aisha, rubbing her hands to warm them and blew through her mouth to maintain her body temperature.

Rohit offered her his jacket and she gratefully accepted. He pulled her closer and made her sit right in front of him, with his hands around her waist. He rested his chin on her shoulder, while Aisha closed her eyes.

"Now how does it feel?" Rohit asked her, kissing her on her cheeks.

"Fantastic! When you're around me, it always feels good," she winked and kissed him back.

They both then talked about their past. Aisha told Rohit about Delhi, her parents and her friends, while Rohit went on with his Pune story. Rohit often had conflicts with his dad. Both of them were poles apart in almost every way and never came to talking terms. He shared many such memories with Aisha. It was the first time both talked their hearts out, about what they felt about the world, about their family, and much more.

"You shouldn't be fighting with your dad," Aisha said to Rohit.

"He is just too much! We have quarrels on the smallest things. He keeps yelling at me, at minor mistakes; he is short-tempered and has the habit of taunting me over just about anything I do or try to carry out; I just hate him," replied Rohit.

"Never say that! After all he is your dad, Rohit. However he might be, you shouldn't shut him out on your part. Somewhere inside him, he does love you. He has given you almost everything. He may be short-tempered, but there is no father in this world who doesn't love his child. You have to love him back and be as kind as you can," Aisha tried to explain to Rohit.

Rohit listened to everything she said but didn't reply.

A cold wind blew and Aisha grabbed Rohit. He curled his arms around her while she rested her head on his chest. He immediately kissed her cheeks and her hair fell on his face. Her hair had a pleasant fragrance. Rohit moved it aside and held her face. Love was in the air. Rohit kissed her neck and made her moan with pleasure. Aisha moved closer to him and gave him a love bite on his neck.

"Ahh," he shouted "What are you doing? It hurts!"

"I know," she showed her teeth "I want the world to know that you're mine and no more single! That mark will tell everyone."

Rohit smiled and kissed her on her forehead. As she moved closer to him, she closed her eyes. The distance between them decreased till they could feel each other's breaths—they kissed each other hesitantly at first, but later got past it. It was their first kiss and the breeze, the cold night, and the peace around with no one to see them, made it a romantic moment for the two. They cuddled each other, soon turning it into a passionate intimacy. The cold brought the two of them more and more close to each other and their bodies kept them warm. Romance was in the air and seemed endless as they continued kissing each other.

***

"Wake up, you two," I said, turning back, when I saw both of them sleeping during the lectures.

I woke them up, but both didn't seem to be in the mood to even raise their heads and look around.

The day dragged for them. Both were drowsy until the semester results were declared. Neha and I passed in Physiology and Biochemistry but failed in Anatomy, narrowly. Aisha passed in all the three subjects, while Rohit flunked in all three.

"Why don't you study?" shouted Aisha, as soon as the results were declared.

"It's not easy. Nothing goes into my brain," replied Rohit.

"That's because you don't even try!" Aisha retorted back, getting serious.

Soon, the principal came in. He gave a long speech about how poor the performance was and threatened everyone that he would inform our parents about our low scores in the exam. He then continued, saying that in case our performance was poor in the prelims, we would be put on the detention list.

The detention list meant that we wouldn't be able to appear for the university (final) exam and would have to give the supplementary exam, which is usually held two or three months later. Amongst the four of us the threat was only applicable to Rohit. Detention list was made on two criteria: one was poor performance while the other was poor attendance. Attendance was no issue for Rohit. He had attended most of the lectures, always with the fear of detention and the supplementary exam.

Aisha gave in all of a sudden, "I am going to teach you from today. We are going to study in the library every single day till our prelims and the final exam. No more movies, no more dinners and roaming around now."

"There's no need for that, dear," replied Rohit, catching her hand and kissing it. "I can manage it on my own," he continued.

"Stop it, Rohit! Be serious sometimes. You've failed in all the subjects and still you refuse to wake up! You know, even if you fail in one subject, you will have to repeat the whole year."

"I won't fail. Don't worry!" He went on kissing her.

"Please! Grow up! Think about it—what if you fail and you have to repeat the year while Aisha, Neha and I step ahead?" I said, as we reached the college canteen for some hot coffee.

"I don't care, you can go ahead, but Aisha should be with me," he teased and then got a little serious thinking about the "what if even Aisha moves ahead"? He didn't speak for a while.

"You hit the target," Aisha laughed.

"That's how it has to be done," I boasted.

***

Days passed and there was a slight change in Rohit. Since the announcement of our semester results, both Aisha and Rohit had started studying together in the library. Rohit didn't like studying at all, but with Aisha teaching him, he started building the bridge between him and studies. The same chapters which he found difficult now seemed easier to him. When Aisha taught him certain chapters he understood it even better than the lectures. During dissection, Aisha taught him the identification of various muscles and organs with their nerve supply, origins, insertions, and actions, explaining each and everything right from the basics. With time, his performance improved. His progress in all the subjects was phenomenal and worth appreciating.

"So, he is progressing in studies with time!" I remarked

once to Aisha, when we were sitting on one of our college campus benches.

"All credits to this girl," Rohit said and kissed her hand.

She smiled, looking into his eyes. Both caught each other's hand while Aisha rested her head on his shoulder. Love was in the air, a pure love and respect for each other.

A smile is the lighting system of the face, a cooling system of the head, and healing system of the heart, which we can get only from a special person. Rohit was getting it all from Aisha and she was the special person in his life. I was happy for him. He had earlier mentioned not being committed to Aisha, but this changed with time. Their love was pure, with no great expectations from each other. They were happy and accepted each other as they were.

"Hey, we have to study Physiology," said Rohit, all of a sudden.

"Look who is talking!" remarked Neha and we all laughed.

Rohit smiled and looked at Aisha and then continued, "You have your Physiology quiz. Let's get going, we have to study."

Aisha got up as Rohit pulled her.

"'Bye, guys," said Rohit, as the two turned away from us.

"We were planning for a movie. Aren't we going for one?" I asked, raising my voice, so that he could hear me as he hurriedly walked away from us.

"No, dude, next time, we have got some other mission

to accomplish today," he replied and his voice faded, the farther he went from us.

"Strange right?" remarked Neha.

"By the way, I have been meaning to appreciate that mark on your neck for a while now—it does look good," I teased him.

Although he was far away from us, we could see him blushing. He tried to hide the love bite under his shirt's collar. Neha and I giggled and again shouted in unison, "Someone's love bite is just too cute!" Rohit turned towards us and saluted us with his middle finger.

"Alright! Go and study in the library, don't come back with another mark," Neha continued teasing him. He didn't respond this time and we gave up.

I knew that Rohit had changed but changing to the extent that he gave more importance to studies than anything else was a shock for me. All credit went to Aisha.

Both of them studied for the Physiology quiz. Rohit asked her questions while she answered them. We had four batches for the quiz. Aisha represented the 'C' batch and along with two other guys had taken part in the intra-college quiz. The best batch would then represent the college for an inter-college quiz. Rohit wanted Aisha to rock in the quiz and was determined to motivate her.

***

Finally, the day of the Physiology quiz arrived. Although Aisha was good in studies and was amongst the favourite students of our college, she was nervous about the crowd who was going to watch her when the quiz took place. She feared the questions that would be asked and was afraid of not being able to answer the questions, and this freaked her out.

"Don't be tensed, dear!" Rohit encouraged her, holding her face in his hands.

She looked at him and their eyes met. Aisha sensed Rohit's love for her. His eyes seem to say, "I am there, don't worry. You have studied well and you will rock."

Even though he didn't speak a word, she could sense what he wanted to say by reading his eyes.

Minutes later, the Physiology quiz commenced. Ten rounds of questions and Batch C began on a low note. They were last on the points table. Rohit was more stressed out than the team members and their mentors. He sat with his fingers crossed. The happy-go-lucky, careless guy had turned serious that day.

"Dude! Why are you so tensed?" I asked him.

"I and tensed, no way!" he replied with some fake laughter.

Not even for a minute did he take his eyes off her. He prayed for her to win. The crowd began commenting on how poorly Batch C was performing. When Aisha couldn't answer some of the questions, the other students in the crowd from Batch C started regretting having sent Aisha to represent their batch.

Everything seemed to be going downhill until the buzzer round began. Aisha took a deep breath and pressed the buzzer for every question. In spite of the risk of getting negative marks for every wrong answer, she pressed the buzzer before any other batches as Batch C was already at the fourth position and had nothing to lose. The first question she answered turned out to be correct. She pressed the buzzer again and the second one went again into her pocket. With the third answer correct, the crowd began cheering for her. Batch C jumped from the fourth position to the second position. Confidence built up in her, she started answering the questions firmly and in a confident tone. At the other end, Rohit relaxed, and his face reflected his joy.

"C'mon!" he shouted with delight, hitting his palm with his fist.

The crowd, which had been cursing some time ago, now had started encouraging Aisha. With the final question she answered, the crowd rose to its feet.

"The answer is correct," our professor said.

Batch C had bagged the first position with the final answer! Rohit jumped off his seat in delight. Everyone started clapping and whistling for Aisha. Some shouted Best-batch-C-batch, while the others just teased the other batches.

As the awards were presented, Aisha was thrilled and so was Rohit. Their combined efforts had proved to be victorious for them. Aisha received a shower of praise from the teachers. She kept an eye on Rohit to read his expressions. He was the happiest person there, jumping in the crowd. Since the day I had met him, I had never seen him this happy.

"We want a party!" said Neha, when we four met, post the quiz session.

"Where do you want it? Just tell me," said a happy Rohit, as he hugged and kissed Aisha on her forehead.

Love between the two didn't diminish; in fact, it grew stronger with every passing second. As time passed, both had started caring for each other and loving each other more than ever. It was time for the final exams. All of us passed. We again partied as we were officially now into the second year.

After a movie, we went out for dinner.

"Here's a bottle of champagne for our success!" Rohit said and opened it and we all cheered.

"It was impossible for me to pass," remarked Rohit, as he sat next to Aisha.

Aisha pecked his cheek.

"Oh, so now do one thing. Let's see how you propose to her," Neha said, sipping some champagne from the glass.

"I have already proposed to her, you idiot!" exclaimed Rohit and laughed over it.

"I mean say something nice to her; dedicate something very romantic on the spot. Let's see how you do it," replied Neha.

All Neha was doing was trying to pull his leg. She elbowed me, when I tried to change the topic.

Rohit instantly went down on his knees and began, "On the canvas of life we often go off colour, but as long as you are there to add the right shades, life will be a rainbow."

Aisha smiled and looked into Rohit's eyes. Her eyes gleamed with joy.

"I wanna go on a road trip someday. I wanna get away and explore different places, sleep in the car, stop to admire the view, visit various beaches, hotels and try out various coffee shops. I want to listen to my favourite albums while driving and click photographs with a Polaroid camera but in all these situations what I want in common to add the right colour to them is you and only you. I made a list of special people in my life with a pencil but when I reached your name, I used a pen because I'm sure that I'll never have to make any change, I love you like hell and I will always love you," continued Rohit in a single breath, without pause.

"Woahh!" exclaimed Neha.

Aisha didn't say a word. She instantly held his head and kissed him on his lips.

"Let's get moving," I said to Neha. She laughed and we walked away to give the two of them some privacy. We came back after a while.

"Sorry!" said Aisha, when we came back.

"No, it is totally fine. You just couldn't control your feelings. We can understand," I teased her and we all burst into laughter. Aisha blushed and her cheeks turned pink.

The main course was soon ordered and we started relishing it. The food was really awesome. On top of it we were hungry, thus adding more dishes to our table.

"How would it be if we all went to Goa? The exams are done, we have holidays and it would be fun. What do you all say?" Rohit asked us, as we paid the bill and made our way to the parking area.

"It does sound exciting, I am in," replied Aisha delightedly, almost leaning over Rohit.

Neha and I didn't respond right away, but with the two convincing us repeatedly, we had to cave in.

CHAPTER 4

One Step Closer

Bags packed, resort booked online, and bus tickets in hand, we set off to Goa. It was an overnight bus journey and we would reach Goa the next day. Two more college friends, Shashank and Kriti, had joined us. Shashank was a friend of ours while Kriti was Aisha's and Neha's friend.

Turning on some music with headphones in our ears, sometimes chatting, sometimes taking a nap, we reached Goa the next morning. We took a cab to the resort.

"Wow, nice ambience, good choice, Rohit!" I exclaimed, as we arrived at the hotel property.

Rohit had planned everything right from the bus tickets to the resort rooms. Every aspect of our trip was taken care of by him and so far, he seemed to have done a great job. The rooms were stupendous and were on the ground floor. The wood gave it a cottage like appearance. We had an amazing view of the beach and could hear the sound of the waves right from our rooms. Once we stepped out, there was sand to welcome us. Nature's breathtaking beauty and sublime skill brought a huge smile on our faces.

Rohit and Aisha checked in to their room, while Neha and Kriti departed to theirs. Shashank and I decided to walk over the sun-kissed sand and dive into the water. Wearing our Torsos and shorts, we both sprang into the water.

***

We had rested during the day, and then, it was evening.

"You're ready?" Shashank asked Rohit and Aisha, knocking on their door.

"Yeah, just a minute," replied Rohit from inside.

It was 6.30 p.m. With the setting sun and the flawless atmosphere around, the resort in-charge had arranged a bonfire for us on our request on the shore. All of us were ready and already gathered, while Rohit and Aisha added a couple of minutes to delay everything.

"Sorry, I know we are late," said Aisha, clenching her teeth as the two came out of their room about fifteen minutes later.

She looked amazing in her black gown. Rohit looked super cool in his grey T-shirt and black three-fourths pants.

The bonfire was lit and we sat around it in a circle. We ordered some beer. Aisha tried to stop us, but with Rohit convincing her and knowing that we were all on vacation, she soon gave in. With glasses filled to the brim, we said "cheers" and took a sip. We turned on some music, and later played Dumb Charades till it was almost 8.30 p.m.

After dinner, Aisha said to Rohit, "Let's go for a walk."

Rohit held her hand and the two set off. The four of us stayed back around the bonfire.

It was full moon, with stars twinkling, and a gentle breeze. Aisha entwined her arm with Rohit's and they walked on the soft sand. Darkness fell, and all they could hear, besides the sound of their own breaths, was the sound of the waves, which got louder and louder as it approached the shore. Each time a wave came, the water would gently kiss Aisha's feet and the wind would blow her hair, making it brush Rohit's face and he would gently move it away. Aisha rested her head on his shoulder and they continued walking. With each step they took, their hearts got closer. With feelings of intimacy, Rohit held her face as she turned towards him. She linked her hands behind his neck and their lips met.

"How lucky the two are! I pray they remain happy always," Neha said as we saw the two walk away from us and fade into the darkness.

"Only a year, yet they seem to have been together since ages. They are the perfect couple, meant to be together for a lifetime. I wish God always keeps them happy," Kriti joined in.

I didn't utter a word. I knew how well the two gelled and wished it to be the same, always. Love was meant for the two of them. No great expectations, no demands, no complaints, the two complemented each other to the fullest.

***

"Open the door! Alok! Shashank!" shouted Neha, banging on the door.

"Yeah, one sec," I replied back in a sleepy voice.

Shashank got up the next moment, rubbing his eyes.

I quickly switched on the lights and checked the time. It was almost 2.30 a.m.

"What happened?" I asked Neha, as I opened the door, running my hand through my hair.

I saw Neha standing there, somewhat tense. Behind her was Aisha, weeping, with Kriti trying to console her. I turned my head to the right and found Rohit leaning against the wall, with his head bent.

"What happened?" I asked again, this time to everyone in general.

Neha stepped inside the room and pulled me aside. The others also entered and seated themselves wherever they could find place in our messy room.

"What happened?" I asked for the third time, now getting a little worked up and fully awake.

Neha then told me everything. A little earlier, Aisha had gone into Kriti and Neha's room crying and complaining about Rohit. Apparently, Rohit was asleep and the phone constantly buzzed with messages. Aisha had checked his phone, to find conversations between him and a girl named Kajal.

When Neha had finished, I said, "Arey, she is his ex-girlfriend," loud enough to grab everyone's attention.

"That's exactly what I am trying to explain," Rohit piped in, in a gloomy but demanding voice.

Aisha got up from her place and handed Rohit's mobile to me. She opened the chat and showed it to me.

I went through the messages where Rohit had continuously complimented Kajal over her dress sense and her beauty. As I scrolled down I found his flirtatious messages. My eyes widened on each and every statement I went through and suspected the possibility of the situation turning nasty.

"What the hell is this, Rohit?" I asked him with a tinge of anger in my tone.

"Bro, I am telling you, she is my ex-girlfriend and there's nothing between us. I swear!" he replied.

He got up from his place and pulled me out of the room.

"Alok, just check the dates. Though she has been messaging me recently, I have stopped responding to it long back, I don't even reply to her," said Rohit, in a convincing tone.

I checked their conversation once again. Rohit hadn't messaged Kajal lately nor had he replied to any of her messages. All the messages we saw were a few months old.

"But why the hell were you flirting with her, a few

months back when you had Aisha in your life?" I asked him in a louder voice.

Rohit remained silent for a while. I repeated the question and he replied, "I wasn't really sure about Aisha then, but now I am! I was just a little confused. I thought it was mere attraction and so always kept in contact with Kajal. I didn't want to lose Aisha, so I never told her about my confusion. Nor did I want to break contact with Kajal. As time passed, I started becoming committed to Aisha, I started understanding that this bond we share is as precious as pearls and that we were meant to be together. She has now become my need and my only life."

"Then why didn't you delete the messages?" I asked him.

"It never occurred to me", he replied, sheepishly.

"I love Aisha! I really love her," continued Rohit.

I thought of a way out of the problem. There was dead silence for a while until I suggested that he go and apologise to her immediately.

He looked straight into my eyes and then started walking back to the room, on shaky legs. As he entered the room, all eyes turned to him. Aisha was still weeping. He walked towards Aisha and put his hand on her shoulder but she immediately shrugged it away. He tried to hold her face but she shook his hands off trying to resist him.

"I am sorry, Aisha," said Rohit, in a low voice.

"These messages aren't recent ones. Yes! Kajal has been messaging me but I don't reply to any of them. There's nothing between us. I love you Aisha and I need you, I swear," continued Rohit.

"You were messaging her, a few months back when we were already in a relationship and what does that mean? This is betrayal. I trusted you but now I can't. I loved you but now I can't and you know why, because you never valued it. I shared my past with you, I told you I had a boyfriend before you, but you lied saying this was your first relationship. You are a liar!" replied Aisha and again burst into tears.

"I am sorry, Aisha! I did not do it on purpose. I love you. She was my past. I know I lied to you about her but that was only because I wanted our relationship to work out. I was madly in love with you, still am, and always will be! So I didn't share my past, fearing it might have affected my future. I am sorry, Aisha!" continued Rohit.

He then deleted all the messages and even blocked Kajal's number but Aisha wouldn't listen. She kept sobbing and started walking out of the room. She stopped at the door, looked back at Rohit and all she said was, "It's over, Rohit!"

Toota ho dil toh dukh hota hai,
Karke mohabbat kisi se ye dil rootha hai.
Dard ka ehsaas tab hota hai,
Jab kisi se mohabbat ho aur
Uske dilme koi aur basa hota hai"

Translation:

It pains when the heart is broken,
The heart is sad in spite of loving someone.

**You feel the pain when you love a person
And they already have someone else in their heart
to make the things worse.**

No matter which path you walk upon or what means you choose, you will definitely succeed in accomplishing your desires, but what's the use? In the longer run only those whose foundations are strong survive. The love of a person can be achieved by any means. A person might lie a hundred times to win someone's love but he will definitely be exposed one day and at that point his real intentions might be revealed. When the other person comes to know about it, it leads to nothing but problems in the relationship.

Rohit's approach had brought on mistrust in his relationship with Aisha and the foundation of their love was shaking. She no longer trusted him. Rohit was in agony and repented his mistake but was now helpless. Aisha too was in agony and couldn't sleep the rest of the night and neither could Rohit. He was worried that he might have lost Aisha forever.

The next morning Rohit went for a walk on the beach by himself as he wanted some time off and declined my offer to accompany him. He was in pain. He walked on the sand and then after sometime sat there for a while. He looked towards the bright sun. The rays kissed his body, illuminating his skin. The sea was calm, which was how he was feeling at that moment. The waves seem to mirror the spreading silence and gloom. Rohit folded his legs and rested his head on his knees, his mind full of thoughts of

Aisha. Suddenly, he felt as if someone was behind him. When he tried to turn back, he felt two arms embrace him from behind. It was Aisha. She hugged Rohit and said, "I am sorry, Rohit! I shouldn't have overreacted."

She paused for a moment and kissing Rohit's cheeks, continued, "You shouldn't have lied. You could have told me everything. I know you flirted with Kajal even when we were in a relationship and that is a form of betrayal. You might still betray me and for this I want to forget you, I want to hate you, I want to curse you. I wish to flush you out of my mind, my heart, my soul, and my body but I don't know why I can't do that. Every second I try to do this my heart stops me. I love you and can't afford to lose you."

Aisha had tears in her eyes. Rohit wiped them and said, "Aisha, I am sorry. Back then, I thought I wasn't committed to you. I had Kajal in my life before you and even after I broke up with her we remained in contact, but it was only during the initial days of our relationship. I found my love in you and became committed to you. Since that day my heart beats only for you. Falling in love is like looking at the stars. I picked you out of the billions and stared at it long enough till all the other stars melted away. I did begin our relationship on the basis of lies but my intentions were not wrong. Later, when I realised what this bond means to me, I thought it would be better to keep my lie concealed, fearing it might affect our relationship, which it eventually did. I know I was wrong. Baby, please forgive me. I love you and never want to lose you."

Aisha immediately hugged Rohit and he hugged her back. She rested her head on his shoulder while he stroked her head with love. Silence enveloped them. The breeze blew Aisha's hair, making the atmosphere romantic. Both looked into each other's eyes and were lost in their love. The calm waves of the sea now began to roar as if cheering each other.

"I love you too," said Aisha, after a while, and Rohit smiled. He kissed her gently on her cheek. It felt as though both had taken a step forward in their relationship—one step closer!

We were happy that Rohit and Aisha's relationship was back on track. Although they fought for less than a day, it felt as if they were back together after a long time.

After breakfast we made our way to Calangute beach. We hired three two-wheelers at a reasonable rate and set off down the beach. Although we were in Goa in the month of July, the sea waves weren't as violent as we had expected them to be. All water sports were shut down but we still got a chance to get into the water.

"Beer?" I asked Rohit, as we reached the shore. There were many alcohol shops where people headed as soon as they got there.

"No," said Rohit, even before Aisha could react.

"My whole body wants except for my heart," he continued.

"Huh?" I gave him a puzzled look

"My heart lives here," he said in a filmy manner, pointing towards Aisha.

Aisha, overjoyed, immediately hugged him and kissed him.

"Thank you, Rohit," she went on.

Looking at them, even I gave up my plan, although Goa and no boozing did seem like a bad idea. Shashank didn't care and he ordered a beer while Neha and Kriti made their way to a round of hookah.

I made myself happy with a cranberry breezer, while Rohit and Aisha sprang into the water. We watched them play. Rohit got his chance to showcase his muscular body, while Aisha with her curves set fire to the water. They both splashed water on each other. Aisha would deliberately splash it on his face and when he would try to catch her, she would swiftly slip away from his hands. Rohit finally succeeded in holding her by her waist and lifted her up in his arms and then threw her down into the water.

After we were done with our boozing, we joined the two. My mini potbelly signalled that it would be wise to enter into the water with my T-shirt on. We played in the water for a while.

Later, we headed to Baga beach, which was considered a separate beach, but this was just a formality. Both Calangute and Baga beach shared a common coast and so the beach proved to be boring for us. We decided to leave and went on to Anjuna beach to watch the sunset, before returning to the hotel. The setting sun, with the waves dashing on the hard rocks along the coast and the cool breeze, made it an exotic place. Obviously, how could we miss out on selfies! Aisha and Rohit posed romantically in some of their photos and immediately updated their Facebook profile pictures.

***

"Let's go to Tito's!" said Shashank, on reaching our hotel.

"What is it?" asked Kriti.

"It's a night club. I just found it on the Internet. Ill book the tickets if you like," he replied.

"It'll be fun. Go ahead, Shashank," said Aisha, in an excited voice. She immediately looked at Rohit and gave him a smile. He was happy to go along with Shashank's idea.

So it was set! Shashank booked three couple tickets online. Later, we got ready for the club.

Rohit looked like a stud in his sky-blue body fit T-shirt. Aisha wore a pink crop top and a black skirt. She looked hot in her outfit. Kriti too had a sexy body and looked ravishing in her party dress.

The club seemed to be the perfect place for those who loved to drink. Shashank, Neha, Kriti, and I as usual made our way to the bar counter, while Rohit just had a breezer and pulled Aisha on to the dance floor. He held her by her waist and pulled her towards him. Their eyes met and Aisha seemed a little shy. Rohit held Aisha's loose strand of hair and tucked it behind her ear. She immediately turned her eyes the other way and smiled. After a while, the music turned loud and both Rohit and Aisha grooved to the beat.

Sweeter than the candies, lovelier than the red roses, cosier than soft toys, that's how special Aisha and Rohit were for each other. They were obviously crazy about each other.

Time flew and soon our vacation came to an end. After visiting the Agoda fort, the Panjim market, Dona Paula, and a few churches, we took an overnight sleeper coach back to Pune.

CHAPTER 5

Can't Live Without You

Love is not about keeping score; it is not about how long you have been together, or how much you have given or received. It's definitely not how many times you have helped each other; it is how much you value each other. Some relationships never get on track no matter how hard you try, while there are relationships whose bonds tighten right from the first moment. Aisha and Rohit's relationship belonged to the latter category. Their love was strong and it had a deep impact on their hearts. They always had love and respect for each other, and this kept increasing with every sunset and sunrise.

The second year of our medical education began. We were well-acquainted with the new subjects that had been introduced to us. We were now posted to clinics and we enjoyed whatever came our way. Clinics meant that we could actually examine patients. Although we were not coming from the so called 'talented lot,' we still managed to perform and learn something in the clinics. Meanwhile, Rohit and I rented a flat, a few miles away from our college. We left our college hostel for which all credit went to Rohit. He wanted extended privacy, which was obviously not possible in the hostel. He often called Aisha to our place and during those times, I said, "Aisha, I"ve got some important work. I'll be back after sometime."

Actually, it was Rohit who instructed me to do so. I did nothing for free and so, always demanded something from Rohit in return.

One fine Sunday, six or seven months into our second year, Aisha, Neha, Rohit, and I were watching a movie in our new flat. The genre was romantic which seemed fine for Aisha and Rohit but was a problem for Neha.

"Can anyone please change the movie? It's boring!" complained Neha, drinking some coke from the bottle.

"No! It's good. You can concentrate on the pizzas," Aisha smirked, pointing towards the Domino's pizza boxes, which we had ordered earlier.

Neha had no choice but to give in. I remained silent for a while. I was busy doing something else.

"What are you doing, Alok? What's so important in that mobile that you can't even raise your head?" asked Neha, in an irritated tone.

"Ah . . . nothing," I replied, with my eyes still glued to my mobile and my fingers busy scrolling. "What is it?"

asked Neha, for the second time, getting up from the sofa. She snatched the mobile from my hand.

"No . . . Wait!" I shouted, but she had already grabbed my mobile.

"Ohh ho! *Kya bat hai*!" Neha winked at me, when she saw what I was looking at.

I was embarrassed. I had been checking out a girl's Facebook profile on my mobile. I had been appreciating her photos.

"Listen, guys! It seems Alok is having a secret crush on someone," Neha continued, teasing me, this time loud enough that even Aisha and Rohit turned their eyes upon me.

Rohit immediately paused the movie and jumped off from his couch. He snatched the mobile to have a look at the girl.

"Ohh *mere sher! Kab se*?" Rohit now joined Neha and teased me.

It embarrassed me even more.

"Who is it?" asked Aisha, with her eyes gleaming with excitement.

I looked at her and very shyly replied, "Kr . . . Kriti!"

"Wow! Lucky girl!" Aisha remarked instantly, which brought a huge smile on my face.

It was the first time I had liked a girl. Never before had I been in a relationship or even paid attention towards girls. People generally labelled me a nerd. I have my own doubts whether giving more importance to studies really makes you a nerd. Kriti was the girl for whom my heart beat. She had been with us on our trip to Goa and that was my first interaction with her. Whenever I saw her my heart skipped a beat and currents passed down my spine. I would keep gazing at her but could never really speak freely with her. I don't know why it happens—a person can interact with millions of girls without hesitation, but when it comes to the girl he loves, it becomes almost impossible. I just couldn't face her. Every time we met and made eye contact, either she or I would look away.

"Should I first slap you or should I hug you?" Aisha scolded me.

"Just look at him! He calls us his friends and doesn't share his feelings with us," Aisha continued this time, frowning.

"I am sorry! It's kind of hard for me. I . . . I . . . love her but then I fear rejection. She is too good for a nerd like me," I replied.

"Yeah, so just fold your hands and don't move your ass and she will be yours! Or else just keep staring at her photos and hope for the best!" Neha went on with sarcasm, pointing towards Kriti's profile picture.

"I know that! But it's not that easy. I need to find some guts," I replied in a tense tone.

"Dude, what am I for?" Rohit dived into the topic and brought a smile on my face.

We then discussed various ways for me to approach Kriti. Everyone tried to encourage me. They gave me the moral support I needed. On one hand, I was happy to have such good friends in my life and on the other hand, I had hopes of succeeding in finding my love in Kriti.

"She is too cute, Rohit," I said for the tenth time, after the girls had left.

"I know, dude!" he replied lying on the bed.

I lay on the bed opposite to his with my eyes glued to my mobile. It was midnight and the lights were off, yet sleep seemed tough for me.

"Just look at this one, her pout looks so sweet," I said, surfing through her photo gallery for almost the hundredth time.

"Hmm," replied Rohit.

"And this one is far better! Her eyes are ravishing. Her spectacles add beauty to those eyes. Her silky hair, milky skin, her lips, her nose, gosh! I am falling for her!"

"Hmm . . . I know," Rohit went on.

"You know, Rohit, when I look at her, I forget the present, I forget the people around me, and I vanish into my very own world of dreams where there are only two people—Kriti and me and no one else! Love, passion, ecstasy, fills my world. There's no hatred, no selfishness, no jealousy, just the two of us!"

"Hmm," he replied for the third time.

I paused and then continued, "The day we went to Calangute beach I just fell for her. She looked sexy with those loose strands of hair and those sparkling eyes. The way she sat around the bonfire with her hands curled around her bent legs made me lose myself into her. Her tiny hands when she held mine, her soft feet that kissed the waves on the shore . . . all made me feel like my heart beat for the hundredth time in a single second. How do we look together? What is your opinion?"

"Hmm . . ." he replied.

"Rohit! How do we look together?" I asked him again. There was no response.

"Asshole, say something!"

I turned on the lights and found him fast asleep. I had been talking to the walls. I smiled at myself. Switching off my mobile data, I drifted off to sleep.

***

Loving Kriti would have taken my life, but when I looked into her eyes, I knew she was worth that sacrifice. You can fall from a bridge, you can fall from a mountain, but the best way of falling is falling in love. I felt something in my heart; it was like a little flame. Every time I saw Kriti, the flame would light up. There is 1 universe, 8 planets, 204 countries, 804 islands, 7 seas, and billions of people, but still my heart told me it was just Kriti. I had one heart that was true, and now it had left me with none, for Kriti now had two.

"Alok, you're taking a lot of time!" said Rohit suddenly when he saw me sitting on my bed daydreaming.

"You have to be quick," he continued.

I knew one has to strike when the iron is hot but for a person like me it is always difficult to predict when the iron is really hot. Rohit was quite helpful. He asked me to flirt with Kriti. Flirting when she was right in front of my eyes was difficult for me, so he asked me to stick to mobile texts. Many times, he himself would message Kriti from my mobile. She had started responding to my messages which made me happy enough to travel to the moon and back. Kriti had no idea that although the emotions were mine, the words in the text messages were framed by Rohit. I always had difficulty in framing sentences, especially romantic ones. I was weak in expressing my feelings.

Rohit would often suggest that I invite her out but I would end up saying things like . . .
- It will be too frank.
- Don't you feel it's a bit too early?
- What will she think, dude?
- She won't like it.
- I will ask her next time.

But Rohit was Rohit! He hardly listened to me and finally one day, I ended up texting her. To my surprise, she did respond with an affirmative text message. I was on top of the world. I thanked Rohit a million times, and kept looking at the mirror, until the mirror itself would have stopped me from looking at it. I went through various shirts and finalising one, I set off to meet Kriti. The whole time we were together, I was excited. All the way to the nearest restaurant, I kept looking at her from the corner of my eye. My joy knew no bounds when I saw she was doing the same! We barely talked but exchanged a lot of unspoken words through our gestures. Whenever our hands touched or her shoulder touched mine while we walked, I had goosebumps. Kriti was a shy kind of girl and on top of it, I was a nerd who always needed a stud like Rohit to help me in the smallest of the ways and push me forward, when it came to talking to girls.

A few more months passed and Aisha, Neha, Rohit, and I were again together chatting in our flat. Inevitably, the topic had to again open up.

"When are you going to propose to her?" asked Aisha.

"After we are done with our M.B.B.S. course," said Rohit, with a laugher, enough for Neha to join in.

"Stop it, Rohit! I am serious," continued Aisha, which made the other two stop laughing.

"Okay, Alok, listen! I have always been bombarding Kriti with some or the other topic which has you in it. Every time we talk about you, I begin praising you and this has made at least a little impact on her. I guess she too won't mind if you shift your gear to the next one," said Neha, after a while.

I looked at Neha and jumped off from my seat. I hugged her delightedly and said, "Thank you, you are the one!"

"Alright, alright!" she said. "You owe me something, may be a small party later on," she went on.

I was ready to do whatever it took to bring Kriti and me closer to each other. A party was nothing for me. I immediately agreed to it.

***

"Alok, it's time for you to propose to Kriti," said Rohit, when it was midnight.

"I know! We had a discussion about it some time back," I replied, stretching on the words "I know."

"So get ready, let's go!"

"What? Now? . . . No way, Rohit!"

"Get up!" He said and pushed me out of my bed.

I came up with many excuses like it wasn't the right time, it was risky at that moment, I don't have the guts, I would propose to her the next day.

All Rohit did was take out a few clothes from my wardrobe and ask me to try them on. After I was done with it, he pulled me out of our flat and made me sit on his bike. He sped to our college all the way talking to Neha over the phone. Aisha and Neha were roommates and Neha had told us that Kriti's room was two rooms away from theirs. Rohit was well aware of Aisha's room and so we thought that it wasn't a big deal finding Kriti's room.

"Get down!" said Rohit, when we reached our destination.

"Rohit, listen! It's not the right time. We can't enter the girls' hostel and if we get caught we might be suspended," I replied, scared.

"Shut up and just follow me!" Rohit ordered.

We didn't bring any flowers or gifts. Rohit was against these for he believed that one's emotions were the most important and there was no need for anything else. Rohit had a look around the hostel's entrance and found two security guards. He immediately pulled me aside. We flattened ourselves against the wall to hide ourselves.

"Let's enter from the main road," he suggested.

There was a road at one end of the hostel which had a huge wall lining it with fencing on top. Usually no security guards ever patrolled in that area and we thought it was the safest way to enter the hostel. All credit went to Aisha for leaking out their security plans. We climbed the wall and found a wired fence. It was tough to cross it. We slowly slid our feet across it and tried to fit in between the two iron wires.

"Shh . . . slowly! Don't make any noise!" said Rohit, as we crossed the wired fencing. Rohit got cut by one of the wires but didn't really care. All he would have to do is take an Anti-Tetanus injection the next day.

"Stick to the wall," Rohit instructed as we passed a small room on the ground floor, probably the warden's room.

"There's Aisha's room," Rohit whispered and pointed towards one where the lights were on.

"How are we going there? Take the stairs?" I asked nervously, as I feared getting caught.

"Are you crazy? Which guy takes the stairs to a girls' hostel? We go climb the pipe," he said in a low tone.

"Pipe! I am not coming," I was panicky and tried to run away but Rohit pulled me back.

"C'mon follow me now," he continued and started climbing up the pipe.

I did as I was told and blindly followed him. We reached Aisha's room in a couple of minutes.

"Which side . . . right or left?" Rohit talked to himself.

"Huh?" I asked him in confusion.

"Kriti's room is two rooms away from Aisha's room but

we forgot to ask whether we head towards the left or the right," he said in a frustrated tone.

"What shall we do now?" I asked him.

Rohit was quiet for some time. He thought of a way out and a minute later, banged on Aisha's window. She opened it the next moment and was shocked to see the two of us hanging on to the pole. She asked us to get into their room and we did as we were told. Neha locked the room door while Aisha shut the window. They had thought we were joking about me proposing to Kriti. We tried explaining and the two eventually believed us. Aisha told us that Kriti's room was two rooms away from theirs, towards the left. We thought it better to enter Kriti's room through the window rather than from the main door just in case there was someone around. Rohit pushed me ahead and asked me to knock on Kriti's window.

"What are you doing here?" asked Kriti in a shock, when she saw me hanging on the pole outside her room.

"Can I come in?" I asked rather loudly and received a knock on my head from Rohit. What if someone heard us?

"Shh . . . Just a second," whispered Kriti and then after checking if her door was shut properly, she let me in. Rohit felt it was better to hang outside, so didn't step into the room.

"Where's your room partner?" I inquired when Kriti switched on the lights.

"She's out of town. Why are you here in the girls' hostel?" She asked me, adjusting her hair.

Wow! I exclaimed to myself. Her untied hair and the

pink pajamas made her look hot. When she wore her black-framed spectacles, it made me fall for her even more. She looked cuter than ever. She asked me for the third time why I was in the girls' hostel but I was tongue-tied and star-struck by her beauty.

"Kr-Kr-Kriti . . . mmm, you know you look very beautiful," I stammered. "I have been always attracted to you. I like your company, I enjoy being with you," I continued.

"So?" she asked, raising her eyebrows and looking expressionless, which made the situation worse for me.

"We kind of complement each other. You know . . . like . . . there are only few people who make an impact on a person. I admire you. The way you talk, the way you walk and behave is something . . ." I kept on speaking, till I was interrupted by Rohit.

"Come to the point, you moron! I can't risk hanging here forever," shouted Rohit.

Kriti was smiling but tried to hide her emotions by biting her lips and looking innocent, as if she had no idea what I was blabbering about.

"Why can't she understand?" I said to myself in a frustrated state.

I took a deep breath. In spite of it being November, I had started sweating. My palms were damp.

"I started liking you ever since I saw you for the first time. The thing is I couldn't really express my feelings for you. I daydream about you. I have started forgetting myself and all I can think of is you. You are the one whose presence lights up my heart. You are the one who makes me feel that this world is a better place to live in. I can't live without you. I am mentally and emotionally attached to you by hundreds of invisible strings. I love you, Kriti, and can't stop thinking of you even for a second. You are the reason I attend all the lectures and I reach our college early and leave late. You are the reason I keep recharging my mobile every alternate day. I want us to be one soul. I love you very much!" I poured out my heart in one go. I said whatever came to my mind and whatever my heart told me to speak.

Kriti blushed. I was still nervous and she had sensed it. She liked my innocence and giggled. She came forward and removed her spectacles. I was still anxious. I felt as if the ground below me had started to move. Then Kriti embraced me and without saying a word pecked me on the cheek. That said it all. I was on top of the world. I felt like dancing. It was a dream come true. Rohit immediately tuned on a romantic song over his mobile and shouted, "Yeaaaaaah . . . Hurray!"

Kriti and I responded in unison, "Shh . . . shut up! Someone might hear us."

Rohit controlled his emotions and stepped inside the room. Soon there was a knock on the door. We were worried it might be someone from the hostel staff but were soon relieved when we heard Aisha's and Neha's voices on the other side of the door. Kriti opened the door and they joined in the celebrations.

CHAPTER 6

Winning Is Not Everything!

These were the best days of our lives. I had Kriti and she was happy to have me by her side. Rohit and Aisha were steps ahead of our newly started relationship. Although Neha was single, she was fine being in the group and never complained. My love and respect for Aisha, Rohit, and Neha had reached a zenith for they had always backed me. I know I may sound a little selfish but because of these three besties, I had Kriti in my life. I thanked the three of them a million times. I was blessed to have them as my friends.

With Kriti and these mad friends around, college life was joyful. We attended some lectures, bunked a few, and went out for movies. Except for Aisha and Rohit, we got drunk at night. Then we roamed around on our bikes, teased people and laughed at our own pranks. Aisha, Kriti, and Neha shifted with us into our rented flat, which made life better for all of us; filled with joy and liveliness. The girls didn't tell their parents about this; no parent would have ever allowed their daughter to share her room with a guy. Life was fun. We would turn on loud music and shout and dance like crazy people, and often, some of the elders in the society would warn us. They cursed us but we hardly cared. Our rooms were always in a mess, with Rohit's room being the worst. His used and unused undergarments would be scattered on his bed or on one of the ropes tied in his bedroom. Aisha would clean his room. She would willingly sort his clothes and put them away.

With such people around me who were always supportive of each other, we all passed the second year and were promoted to the third year. In medical college, the term 'year' is a misnomer as the second-year spans one-and-a-half years while the third year is divided into two: Part I and Part II, each one-year long. Sometimes we even denote our education year by semesters. It is quite confusing for non-medical people to understand. So, we often end up explaining this to almost every non-medical person who asks about our curriculum.

***

"Let's take part in the singing competition," Aisha suggested to Rohit, who was busy playing 'Angry Birds.'

"Which competition?" asked Rohit, without looking up, still engrossed in the game.

"Our college competition!" said Aisha, stretching on the sentence.

"No way, I can't sing!" exclaimed Rohit.

"We can at least try! I am a trained singer and you have a magical voice, it will be something challenging," replied Aisha with delight and pulled Rohit out of his bed.

Both Rohit's and Aisha's voices were magical. Everyone tends to exercise those vocal cords when in love and assumes that they are the best singers, but eventually turn out to be bathroom singers for the others. These two were different. They had alluring voices and did complement each other really well. They also had the talent to compose poems. Although composing songs was not their forte, they tried their best but it didn't really work out. Finally, they decided to sing a popular song. A rock band was formed, with a couple of our college mates joining in. Shashank was going to play the guitar while Vikrant would showcase his talent with the drums.

"Well it goes this way," Aisha guided Rohit and sang a few lines from the song. Rohit tried his best to imitate her. He struggled as he wasn't a trained singer. On the other hand, Aisha helped him whenever he made a mistake. It was an inter-college competition and the burden of representing the college on a bigger platform made Rohit quite nervous. With a number of entries already on the list from our college, the committee in charge of extra-curricular activities had set

Winning Is Not Everything!

up an elimination round in which a single group would be selected as the final choice.

The two of them, along with Shashank and Vikrant, practised for hours together every day. Aisha took a lot of precaution when it came to maintaining a good voice. She took care of her vocal cords by giving up sweets and ice-cream. She would even gargle thrice a day. She desperately wanted to win in the competition. Rohit would often end up stating, "I can't make it; you pair up with some other guy. With me by your side, we will definitely lose." Aisha was adamant with her decision and wanted only Rohit to sing with her. She kept encouraging him.

Finally, the day of the elimination rounds arrived and the teams had to prove their singing talent in front of our college committee. Rohit was nervous but Aisha boosted his confidence convincing Rohit to believe in himself. There were four teams. Rohit and Aisha's performance was second. After the first performance which was a complete washout, Rohit and Aisha went on stage with some confidence. Somehow, both felt it wasn't as tough as they had expected it to be. They gave their best. One by one all the performances came to an end to a big round of applause from the committee in charge. The judges had a discussion amongst themselves and announced the results.

"We liked all the performances but it is sad that we must select only one out of the four teams and eliminate the rest. After much discussion, we have come to the conclusion . . ." said one of the committee members and abruptly stopped to increase everyone's heartbeat.

He went on, "We have come to a conclusion that amongst all the teams, one team which outshone the rest is team Aisha and Rohit."

"Did he just call out our name?" Rohit asked Aisha, shocked.

"Congratulations to your team. Aisha you have a magical voice. Shashank you hit the right chord with your guitar, Vikrant you were fabulous with your drums. Rohit you were good in parts but you do have to work a little on the high notes. You can manage it with some practice," said the committee members, greeting the team in private.

All of them nodded in agreement and thanked the committee members for finding them worthy of representing our college in the inter-collegiate singing competition. All the team members were excited.

"Let's party," said Vikrant, once they came out of the auditorium.

"No, no way," replied Rohit. "I have to work on my singing. You people can go if you want to."

"Vikrant, are you crazy? The competition is just fifteen days ahead. We can't afford to waste time," Aisha complemented Rohit.

Vikrant had to finally give in.

"I want all of you to gather for the practise at 5.00 p.m. sharp," Aisha went on, getting serious.

She was the leader out of the four for she was an experienced singer.

"Alright! We will be there," said Shashank and Vikrant in unison and set off home after a while.

"I am sorry, Aisha. I couldn't sing well today," said Rohit in distress.

"It is okay, Rohit, we can practise and we will succeed. Don't worry, dear, no one is perfect here. I'll teach you," replied Aisha, looking into his eyes.

"It's not possible. I won't be able to make it," continued Rohit, with his negativity.

"Didn't we succeed in our studies? Didn't we strive hard that time? It is just the same—think positive and we will definitely win. I am there by your side and just like we succeeded in my Physiology quiz and you passed the first year, we will do the same with singing. We just have to repeat history."

That brought a smile on Rohit's face. Aisha too smiled and hugged him.

The two started practising right away for the competition. They were so engrossed and dedicated in their practise session that they forgot to eat.

After a while, the two sat on the living room sofa. Kriti, Neha, and I were out. Rohit picked up the guitar and started playing it.

"What are you doing?" Aisha asked him.

"Shh . . . This one is for you. I have composed it," replied Rohit and strumming the chords, started singing in a melodious voice.

"When I saw you first, I soared up into the sky,
My dreams with you were flying high.
I don't know, baby, how, when and why,
But everything happened in the blink of an eye."

Aisha smiled and blushed when Rohit held her face. He placed the loose strands of her hair behind her ear and went on.

> **"Looking at your cute face, I missed my heartbeat,**
> **Beautiful eyes with pink cheeks, you**
> **made me forget what to speak.**
> **'Found my angel' I said with a sigh!**
> **Yes, it happened in the blink of an eye."**

Rohit looked into Aisha's eyes. She had tears of happiness. She held his arms and rested her head on his shoulder. Looking into his eyes, she kissed him on his cheeks.

"You are really special, you are the best person in my life," said Aisha, looking into his eyes and fidgeting with his hair.

Rohit kissed her hand and continued,

> **"One look from you makes my day,**
> **And I wonder what I should say.**
> **The way you smile makes me fly,**
> **Yeah . . . It all happened in the blink of an eye."**

Rohit gently pulled at her cheeks, bringing a smile on Aisha's face, which then made Rohit fly high, just like he had described in his song.

**"I then decided, that you were the one,
And made you mine like a moon for the sun,
We'll be the best and rise up high,
Because it all happened in the blink of an eye!"**

"How romantic! I love you, Rohit. I love you so much. You have made my day, you are the best," Aisha poured out her heart.

"Thank you, God!" she said to the Almighty with tears in her eyes. She believed in the Almighty and kept on thanking him a hundred times.

"I am speechless," she went on and hugged Rohit. He hugged her back. He wiped off her tears and kissed her on the forehead. As both of them drew closer to each other, the bell rang and Rohit had to go open the door. He looked pissed when he saw me along with Kriti and Neha. We stepped inside as he opened the door.

"What happened?" I asked Rohit.

Aisha got up from the sofa with her hair in a mess.

"What will happen when a person barges in, while someone is getting cosy?" shouted Rohit, looking frustrated.

Aisha couldn't control her laughter and neither could Kriti and Neha.

"Chill!" exclaimed Neha and patted on Rohit's shoulder.

"May be next time," Kriti teased him.

I still didn't understand what was going on. Then I realised I had turned out to be the rain on Rohit's parade and apologised to him hiding my laughter.

***

"Now where the hell is Vikrant!" exclaimed Aisha, frustrated.

"Only three hours left for the competition to begin," continued Aisha in distress.

Aisha, Rohit, and Shashank had already reached the venue for the singing competition. It was 1.00 p.m. and the competition was due to start at 4.00 p.m. Vikrant was still missing, and this made the three of them worry. Vikrant played the drums and none of the three could replace him. Although there was time for the competition to begin, the three couldn't practise for the final time. Each one of them tried calling Vikrant over the phone but he didn't respond to any of the calls.

"Where the fuck has he disappeared?" complained Rohit, in an irritated voice. He had called Vikrant for the third time and got no response.

"Calm down, people," said Shashank. "He will come, don't worry."

Before Shashank could complete his sentence, Rohit went out of the room. He walked through the corridors, went up to the main gate and then headed back. His anger shot up when he saw no signs of Vikrant.

"Let's practise, just forget about him," said Aisha when Rohit returned.

"Without Vikrant?" questioned Rohit.

"We have no choice, guys, the show must go on," said Aisha, with a sigh.

"You know, we can't perform without him. Who is going to play the drums?" continued Rohit.

"I said we have no choice!"

"Let's change the song, we will sing something melodious which doesn't really need rocking background music," suggested Rohit in distress.

"Don't act childish, Rohit! We can't afford to change the song. We have practised a lot and we can't start afresh just before the competition."

"You know the song needs a drummer and we don't have one!" complained Rohit.

"I know! Let's just go according to our initial plan. All we can do now is hope that Vikrant turns up well in time. Now no more talking, let's practise," replied Aisha.

"C'mon, guys! Shashank pick up the guitar and Rohit come here and start singing," continued Aisha, after a while.

The three were left with no choice but to practise on their own. Rohit started singing and Aisha joined him while Shashank played the guitar. The song they were singing didn't sound good enough as the drum beats were missing in the music. As they were performing, Shashank's mobile buzzed. He saw 'Vikrant calling' displayed on his screen and answered.

"Where are you man?" screamed Shashank.

Aisha immediately snatched the mobile from Shashank's hand and asked Vikrant in a frustrated voice, "Where the hell are you?"

Vikrant: My mobile was on the silent mode, sorry guys!

Aisha: I am asking where have you been.

Vikrant: I'll be there before the competition, don't worry.

Aisha: When will you be here?

Vikrant: At 4.00 p.m.

Aisha: Are you insane? The competition is at 4.00 p.m. How the hell are we going to practise before it?

Vikrant: We have practised a lot, Aisha, no need now!

Aisha: Performance on stage is different, Vikrant! With the entire crowd watching us, I don't want anyone of us to mess up. So, I want you here within the next five minutes.

Vikrant: Sorry, Aisha! I won't be able to come. It's my girlfriend's birthday today. I have to spend some time with her.

Aisha: Man! You can go out with her later. How can you afford to risk our performance like this? It is so childish of you!

Vikrant: I had promised her—sorry, Aisha! I can't come right now. As it is, I've practised a lot and even the committee members of our college have applauded me for my performance. So, don't you worry, I remember everything and will be able to perform well.

Rohit snatched the mobile from Aisha's hand and started speaking in a louder voice.

Rohit: Look, Vikrant! This competition is very important for Aisha and so it becomes important for me as well. If you ruin this competition it won't be good for you. I might sound rude, but yes for Aisha's sake and happiness, I can't bear your reckless attitude. So you'd better be here in time.

Vikrant: Chill, dude! I'll be there and don't worry, we will win.

After exchanging a few more heated words, the two hung up.

"Let's continue with our practice," suggested Aisha and the two joined in.

Rohit gave his best while Aisha's voice as usual sounded alluring. Her voice was so appealing that everyone would want more. Shashank too left no stone unturned, when it came to hitting the right chords on his guitar. In no time the clock struck four and the participants were called into the hall where the competition was scheduled to commence. Rohit, Aisha, and Shashank were ready to rock but waited for Vikrant to turn up. Rohit wore a black leather jacket to add style to his performance. Meanwhile, Aisha tried calling Vikrant a couple of times, who finally arrived.

"Sorry, friends, there was a lot of traffic," Vikrant apologised, applying gel to his hair and combing it.

"You remember the beats, don't you?" asked Aisha.

"Yes, don't you worry," Vikrant assured us.

Kriti, Neha, and I soon reached the venue. As we took our seats, I switched on my camera to click some pictures of these precious moments. Soon, the hosts welcomed the audience. A welcome dance was organised and the performance made us rise to our feet. After the welcome speech by one of the committee members, the contestants were called on stage. The audience represented and supported different colleges from Pune. So, we had a somewhat tough competition. We believed and prayed that our team would perform well and outshine the rest.

The first team was called on stage and they gave a power-packed performance. It was followed by a couple of other teams. Few were worth appreciating and made us groove on the music, while the rest somehow made us fall asleep. With more than twenty teams, Rohit and Aisha's performance was fifteenth on the list. When their names were announced, we were on the edge of our seats.

"C'mon Rohit, Aisha," cheered Kriti.

The lights went off and Shashank started playing the guitar. With the melodious music, Rohit and Aisha made an entry.

"Rohit, Rohit . . . Roooohit!" cheered the girls of our college.

Rohit was the girls' favourites. He looked super-cool in his French beard and black leather jacket. Soon, Vikrant started playing the drums and Rohit and Aisha began to sing. With their alluring voices, the crowd was on its feet.

Aisha's voice was magical but Rohit had practised rigorously and attracted the masses. I clicked a couple of photos while the girls just couldn't take their eyes off Rohit. Our team was definitely performing well and that made us feel proud. With the two being the apple of our eye, all the supporters from the crowd waved our college flags in joy. The crowd was an unbelievable scene of jubilation. We were happy with their performance until there was a sudden change in the music. The lyrics of the song and the background music somehow did not seem to synchronise. Rohit looked at Vikrant and Shashank. Rohit's expression indicated that there was some problem out there. Aisha continued singing, trying to act normal. I glanced at the judges and they seemed to be disturbed by the fact but still kept a smiling face. All of a sudden, the crowd that had been cheering for a while, disheartened by the team's weak performance, continued to wave the flags.

When Rohit and Aisha's performance ended, the crowd appreciated it with a few fake smiles and applause. Rohit wasn't happy with their performance and his frustration was obvious. Aisha kept a cheerful face, pretending nothing had happened.

"What happened?" Aisha asked Rohit, when they went backstage.

"Nothing," he replied, dejected.

"It's okay, we tried our best," said Aisha, with a hand on his shoulder.

Rohit looked into her eyes for a while and then turned the other way.

"This happened just because of you, Vikrant," shouted Rohit, almost dashing into him.

"I am sorry, I am really sorry, I just got carried away by the crowd who were cheering us," he apologised.

"Had you not wasted time with your girlfriend and shown some seriousness, the situation would have been different," shouted Rohit, with his anger rising.

"Your overconfidence has spoilt everything," he continued.

"I am sorry, guys," apologised Vikrant, for the second time.

"Ohh, get lost with your sorry. Before I slap you, just get lost," Rohit turned red hot.

Aisha and Shashank came to Vikrant's rescue before the two of them could get into a fist war. Aisha tried consoling Rohit, who had lost his temper.

"We aren't going to make it, we won't even get to the third position," complained Rohit.

"Doesn't really make a difference, dear, we both tried our best, just forget about the outcome. We practised, we sang, we enjoyed our part, and that is more than sufficient. You did a fantastic job today, what else do you want?" replied Aisha.

"And what about the trophy?"

"Winning and getting into the first three positions isn't everything in a competition. You gave your best and I am happy for you."

"But what's the use when we won't be appreciated for it?"

"Who said we won't be appreciated? The results are yet to be declared and even if we don't win, we have achieved something."

"And what is that something?" asked Rohit.

"Had we not dared to participate in the competition, we wouldn't have known that you have a magical voice—that's something we have gained," Aisha paused and then hugged Rohit and said, "Now cheer up and let's just forget everything."

Aisha had a positive approach to everything in life. She was the kind of girl who believed in striving hard to accomplish her goals, but if somehow, they were not fulfilled, she would not repent. Instead, she would take away something positive out of it. She believed that a problem is not the problem, the problem is the attitude towards the problem.

Once the performance was over, it was time for the results. All the teams were gathered there, some happy, some sad, and some nervous. Aisha and Rohit fell into the happy category. The crowd that had been supporting our college seemed low. There was an air of despondency.

"Third position goes to college St. X*****", said the chief guest. "And the second goes to A*****, while the first one goes to J**** college, congratulations to you all", continued the chief guest.

Our college had failed to bag any of the top three positions but still, Aisha and Rohit were happy, while Vikrant was morose. They congratulated the winning teams and then met us. Kriti, Neha, and I greeted them cheerfully.

Definitely, Rohit had proved his singing abilities and Aisha, as always, had rocked. If Vikrant had not messed up, the situation might have been different. But in the end, as Aisha had rightly said, winning isn't really everything!

***

Aisha and Rohit left for a dinner date. Meanwhile, Kriti and I went for a movie. I bought the tickets and we sat down to watch the movie. I was mesmerised by Kriti's looks. She was slim and had the perfect curves to drive anyone crazy. We were at a VIP theatre that had the best seating arrangements. The seat was spacious and designed like a reclining sofa—practically like a mini-bed. There was a common lamp between two seats which made the theatre a perfect place for couples. As the movie started, Kriti moved closer towards me and rested her head on the common pillow we were sharing. I had my arm around her and held her firmly. The theatre was dark. I turned on the lamp and the light illuminated our faces. Kriti looked into my eyes and I gazed back into hers. Her red lipstick over her soft lips, her milky skin, pink cheeks, and her soft tiny fingers entwined with mine added to the romance. She looked more beautiful and dazzling than ever. Her touch and our eye contact brought an ecstasy I cannot describe in words. The film was boring and the theatre was empty as the film had already been declared a huge flop. We enjoyed the moment and the quality time we had together. Deep in my heart there was a whisper . . .

When I am with you, I feel so fine,
Because now I can call you mine.
I found a love I never knew before,
And I keep loving you more and more.
I sometimes feel I did get so lucky,
That I have someone so nice and pretty,
Stay close to me and never go far
Because I love you just the way you are!

Love knows no reason, no time. It has only one intention: bringing people together to a time called forever. A romantic song was being played in the movie and with one hand, I untied Kriti's hair, while with the other, I gently removed her spectacles. I moved closer to her. We could both sense the warmth of our breath. Our bodies touching each other sent a wave of bliss into our hearts. She tilted her head and closed her eyes, while my lips found hers. We kissed passionately.

Mili naa kabhi itni khushi tumse pehle,
Aisi toh na thi zindagi tumse pehle,
Tumse mile toh jaana mohabbat ko,
Naa samjhe the aashiqui tumse pehle,
Meri har khushi har bat teri hai,
Saanson mein chupi ye haayat teri hai,
Do pal bhi nahi reh sakte tere bin,
Dhadkano ki dhadkti har awaz teri hai.

(I wasn't so happy before you,
Life wasn't the way it is, before you,
I met you and understood love,
Wasn't aware of love, before you,
My happiness lies in you,
Every breath of mine wants you,
Cannot live a second without you,
Every heartbeat of mine speaks for you.)

"I love you, Kriti," I said, after some time.

"I lost my heart to you from the day you came into my life. You are the one who has become more important to me than anyone else. I love your eyes that show a shadow of me inside them, your touch makes me feel I always have you by my side. You are the most beautiful girl I have ever seen. You are everything to me. Thank you, Kriti, for coming into my life," I continued, which brought happy tears into Kriti's eyes. I wiped them away, lovingly.

She smiled and said, "Thank you, Alok. You are really special to me. I never believed in love but you made me fall for you."

She hugged me and I hugged her back.

I won't say I'll never make you cry,
But I'll make you smile before your tears get dry,
I won't say I'll never tell you a lie,
But if I do, I do it for a reason and someday I'll
definitely tell you why,
I don't say we'll never have a fight,

**But I'll always say I'm really sorry when
I realise you were right,
I don't say life together will be easy and bright,
But when things get tough I'll hold you tight!**

***

"So, when is the party?" Neha asked Rohit when he showed us his new Honda City car. His father had gifted it to him and he was thrilled. He was the only one in the college who owned both a bike and a brand-new car. He felt the value of his parents in his life for the first time. They had always loved him and cared for him, providing him with the best facilities.

"Anytime when you all say," replied Rohit, smiling.

Time was no issue for us. We immediately surfed the internet for good restaurants and quickly finalised one. Aisha took the front seat while Kriti, Neha, and I squeezed in at the back.

"Do you have a license?" inquired Neha, before we set off.

"Of course, I have!" he smirked, looking at Neha through the mirror.

"Show me," she went on.

"I have!"

"Then show me! I don't want to break any traffic rules, you've got to show me your license," said Neha, tapping Rohit on his shoulder.

Rohit had to finally show his license and after Neha had

read the details for almost the tenth time, we set off. Rohit accelerated as we drove on to the main road. He shifted his gears and the speedometer responded. He dodged quite a few people and turned on some music. Neha feared overspeeding and asked him to slow down. Whenever Neha convinced him to decrease the speed, he purposely increased it and laughed at her frightened expression. I giggled all the time and Neha elbowed me to convince Rohit to slow down. Finally, Aisha convinced Rohit and he immediately listened to her.

"Thank you, Aisha!" remarked Neha and I couldn't resist laughing, when I saw her face.

We reached our destination and made our way to the dining table. We went through the menu and placed our order.

Kriti sat opposite me. She had been the quietest till then, happy to be a spectator and laughing at our jokes. She was enjoying it and each time she laughed or even smiled my heart went haywire. The red one-piece she wore with the perfect beaded necklace made her stand out from the rest. Her eyeliner made her look ravishing. I just couldn't control my emotions and grabbed her hand under the table. Our eyes met. It was the perfect moment to get lost into a world meant for just the two of us. This pleasant ride of emotions and eye contact was soon interrupted when the waiter served us the Chicken Reshmi Kebab we had ordered. It looked mouth-watering and the moment the waiter left, we started eating with gusto, as if we had not eaten for ages.

We didn't care about the bill as it was Rohit who was paying. We were his friends and when you have a friend paying the bill, who cares! We were purposely extravagant. It's fair in true friendship!

"You have made a hole in my wallet," complained Rohit, when I asked him for a dessert treat after we got back into the car.

"We did it on purpose!" giggled Aisha.

"Even your turn will come," replied Rohit to everyone in general, maintaining a smug smile on his face.

"Stop the car!" shouted Aisha, all of a sudden.

"What happened?" inquired Rohit.

"Look there," she said and pointed towards a mass who danced on the road, enjoying some political leader's victory.

"You just gave me a heart attack," shouted Rohit.

"Sorry!" Aisha bit her lips.

"Let's go and dance with the mob," continued Aisha, her eyes gleaming.

I had assumed Rohit to be the craziest of the lot, but Aisha was a step ahead. The car immediately came to a halt and both got off, moving their bodies with the people on the street. Most of those dancers seemed to be uneducated spoilt brats who didn't know a single word about politics. Like mad men, they mindlessly stretched their vocal cords and danced on the road to some of the cheapest songs we would have never imagined existed.

"Do they even know why they are dancing?" asked Kriti.

"A political person might have won some election and these are his men enjoying his victory as if they have won some important battle. Half of them actually don't know the real reason why they're celebrating, I can bet on that!" I replied and laughed at the sight of the crowd swaying. Many of them were high and not in their senses. We cracked jokes as we watched them.

"Isn't this blocking the roads and creating a traffic problem?" complained Neha, when she saw the traffic jam created by the on-road DJ party.

"This is India! We can't really complain about it. Just enjoy it," I winked.

Meanwhile, Aisha and Rohit were busy having fun. They danced to the music, all the time imitating the mob, actually teasing them in their very own dance style. Neither of the two were aware of the songs being played but kept dancing. Soon, the mob surrounded them.

Some people cheered, "Raje *sahebancha Vijay aso*! (May Raje Sir win)" and celebrated the political leader's victory. Aisha and Rohit joined them, totally unaware of what was happening.

"Just look at him!" said Kriti, pointing towards a person who danced with a handkerchief around his neck and the first three buttons of his shirt open, enough to expose his sweaty hairy chest.

Neha couldn't control herself and burst into laughter. Meanwhile, I just couldn't resist walking towards the guy and imitating him, enough to create the false impression that he was the best dancer out there. Rohit and I joined the guy while Aisha made a video of our dancing skills. Rohit switched to a 'Nagin dance' and I joined him. The guy too went on his knees and showed us his moves. The scene was so comic that the girls sitting in the car laughed their hearts out.

CHAPTER 7

Meeting the Parents

A year later . . .

We had completed four–and-a-half years of our M.B.B.S. course and were on the threshold of our internship. It meant we would practice medicine as doctors in our college, seeing and treating patients. We were posted to different departments. Although there were no theory lectures and no practicals, we had to study for the upcoming post-graduation examinations. The nightmare of facing the same competition just as we had in our M.B.B.S entrance exams made us shudder. While we pursued our M.B.B.S course from a private college, showed off about how our college was better, and tried to prove how different we were from others, our false beliefs had actually changed. Government colleges were way ahead of the private ones; after all there is no alternative for the best. We now dreamt of getting into a government college. This meant working hard and we were ready to do whatever it took. There was one year left to prepare for the exam and we were all set to get the ball rolling.

Aisha was going to Delhi for a few days. Rohit had decided to accompany her. The two of them had taken a week's leave of absence. Aisha informed her parents that she was bringing a friend. Although Rohit had agreed to stay at her place, he couldn't find the courage to confront her parents as he was meeting them for the first time. The two of them took a morning flight.

"I am tense," said Rohit, when the two of them walked out of the airport.

"Don't worry, dear, my parents aren't demons, they won't eat you up," joked Aisha, laughing.

"And you are my friend and not my boyfriend when we are here," continued Aisha and winked at him.

"I know! Still I am afraid."

"It doesn't sound good to be your friend," continued Rohit with laughter.

"Aisha!" someone shouted from the crowd.

It was Aisha's cousin Soham. He was very happy to see Aisha after ages and so was she. Aisha immediately rushed to him and hugged him tightly. "Soham *bhaiya*, this is Rohit, my college friend," Aisha introduced Rohit and Soham. Rohit shook hands and the three of them then got into Soham's car.

"Bhaiya, I didn't expect you today, how come you are here?" asked Aisha.

"When my lovely sister is coming home, how can I not spare a day for her?"

"Aww . . . Thank you, bhaiya, love you." Aisha hugged him again.

Rohit, on the other hand, was feeling uncomfortable and sat next to the driver, as Aisha and her cousin got into the backseat of the car. With Aisha busy catching up with Soham, he felt somewhat left out. With no one to talk to, he sat in silence. Aisha sensed Rohit's discomfort and initiated a common topic that the three of them could be a part of. Soham asked Rohit about his life, his studies, and his family. Rohit tried to be as polite as he could. Soham appreciated it and instantly took a liking to Rohit.

"Bhaiya, I want to have Biryani at Kajeez's, let's go there," said Aisha.

Soham told Aisha that her parents were dying to see her but Aisha didn't listen.

"Are you fine with it?" Soham asked Rohit, "You might be tired," he went on.

"Ahh, not at all a problem, anything is fine with me," replied Rohit.

Soham and Aisha again started chatting and Rohit felt like running away but that was obviously not an option. He whispered to the driver to turn on the radio. Hardly a minute had passed when Soham asked the driver to reduce the volume.

"*Band hi kar do!*" continued Soham, a minute later.

Rohit sighed. They had been travelling for almost an hour and still there was no sign of the restaurant or Aisha's house. Rohit decided to strike up a conversation with the driver.

"*Delhi achha hai!* (Delhi seems to be a good place!)"

"*Aap kabse hai Delhi mai?* (How long have you been in Delhi?)"

"*Aaj garam hai temperature, ya fir har din aisa hi hota hai?* (Is the climate hot today or is it always like this?)"

"*Pune aaye ho kabhi?* (Have you ever been to Pune?)"

"*Car mileage kitna deti hai?* (What's the mileage of this car?)"

The conversation was meaningless, but the driver replied to him, constantly chewing his tobacco.

"Here we are!" exclaimed Soham, when they finally reached Kajeez's biryani house.

Thank God! thought Rohit to himself, relieved.

The three of them made their way into the restaurant. The hotel manager greeted both Soham and Aisha as he knew them well. They sat at their table, with Soham sitting next to Aisha and Rohit opposite to Soham. Aisha ordered her biryani and Soham invited Rohit to have a look at the menu.

"I'll have a biryani too," replied Rohit, without going through the menu.

Soham went to the counter to place the order. Rohit burst out, "I am also here with you, Aisha! Don't make me feel like a stranger."

"What did I do?" asked Aisha.

"Your cousin is so boring! He doesn't even know how to make your guests feel comfortable," complained Rohit.

"Sorry, are you bored?" went on Aisha and laughed looking at Rohit's expression.

"Of course, you idiot!"

"Ohh, sorry my baby," Aisha again laughed. "Soham isn't that bad," she went on.

"Oh! Really? I don't think so," replied Rohit in frustration.

Rohit wanted to continue the conversation but stopped when he saw Soham returning to the table.

***

Man! Her parents are good but her cousin is fucking crazy!" said Rohit, over the phone.

I laughed at the other end.

"You are laughing! Disgusting man," he continued.

"You were keen on meeting her parents and staying at her place, now face it," I said, laughing.

"Six more days, man! I'd better die now," he laughed at the other end.

We talked for a while and then after motivating him, I hung up. When it was almost nine, Aisha dashed into the guest room.

"Dinner is ready, Rohit! Come down," she said.

"Why are you sitting here?" continued Aisha.

"Go enjoy yourself, make me feel like a stranger," taunted Rohit.

"Ohh, I am sorry, dear. I have come here after a year; I am just getting carried away with my family."

She quickly hugged Rohit which was enough to change his mood. Rohit splashed water on his face a couple of times and looked into the mirror. He then accompanied Aisha to the dining table.

"*Beta*, sit here," said Aisha's mother, offering him a seat at the head of the table.

Everyone took their seats except Aisha's mom, who preferred to serve the food.

"So, how do you find M.B.B.S.?" asked Aisha's father, who himself was a gynaecologist.

"Uncle, medical life is tough but still manageable if one has the passion," replied Rohit, politely, putting rajma and roti in his mouth and then carefully wiping it with a handkerchief.

"Well said!" exclaimed Aisha's dad. "So, what do you dream of pursuing after your post-graduation?"

Rohit was silent for a while. He had never thought about it.

"Uncle, I'd like to become a gynaecologist," replied Rohit, thinking of impressing Aisha's dad.

"That's great, son! Gynaecology is the best department," said Aisha's dad, as he always had the tendency to boast about his own medical branch.

"Dad, can we talk something else? We don't want medicine discussions on our vacation; we have had enough in our college," Aisha exclaimed, when she found Rohit stuck in the awkward situation.

She knew Rohit better than anyone else there. He was not the studious type and didn't really enjoy discussing studies.

"Have this *dal tadka*," said Aisha passing the bowl to Rohit.

"I hope it is good," laughed Aisha's mom. "Aisha made it."

Rohit glanced at Aisha who smiled back at him. Before he could even taste it, he expressed how much he loved it. It made Aisha smile and show off her cooking expertise. She had cooked something for the first time in her life. Though the tadka was a bit on the lower side, Rohit relished it.

"May I have another bowl of dal?" asked Rohit, after he had finished the first one. He was rewarded by the huge smile on Aisha's face.

***

After a couple of days, Rohit contemplated heading back home. Although he had planned to spend almost a week in Delhi, he found it awkward both for him and for Aisha's family. Since he was meeting them for the first time he was a little uncomfortable. It was 8.00 p.m. It occurred to him that it might be better to leave for Pune the next day. He informed Aisha about it. Aisha wasn't happy with his plan but he insisted that it wasn't right for him to stay at her place for more than two days.

"What will your parents think?" asked Rohit.

"They won't think anything and they are my parents

and not yours, why are you so worked up about it?" replied Aisha, frowning. Rohit thought it made her look cuter than ever.

He was adamant about leaving, though. He had made up his mind. It was just a matter of four or five days of being apart from each other but Aisha was not pleased about it.

When the two sat at the dining table for dinner, Rohit informed Aisha's parents about his departure. They insisted that he stay back a couple of times before giving up.

"Mom, can we spend a day out tomorrow? I think he is bored over here," Aisha sought her mother's permission.

Her mom didn't mind. It made Rohit re-think his decision. The thought of roaming around Delhi with his girlfriend was suddenly exciting. He had been pretending to be her friend in front of her parents for the last two days and was definitely missing the intimacy he shared with Aisha. He felt as if his freedom had been snatched away, compelling him to live in some kind of invisible prison.

"Yes, beta, stay here for a day; have a look at our Delhi as well, it's better than Pune," joked Aisha's mom, smiling.

Rohit liked her. He immediately agreed and that pleased Aisha.

"Even I will join you two," added Soham.

Son of a bitch! thought Rohit. *He had been quiet all this while and when I decided to stay back, only to spend a day with my girlfriend alone, why the fuck did he have to join us?* continued Rohit with his thoughts.

He felt like crying. Soham had again rained on his parade. "Why, man, why?" he said to himself.

Aisha glanced at Rohit's face and giggled over his pissed look.

"What happened?" Aisha's mom asked her.

"Nothing!" she replied, biting her lips to control herself from laughing.

On the other hand, Soham was super excited and said, "So, we leave tomorrow morning after breakfast and head first to India Gate, then to Birla temple and at last to Red Fort."

Rohit kept quiet and repented over his decision to stay back.

"Or maybe even for shopping," continued Soham.

Chup baith, ch**iye! Rohit wanted to say.

After a long discussion, Rohit found it better to escape, as he just couldn't tolerate Soham. He wished Aisha goodnight and returned to the guest room. He was furious with Soham. He didn't like him and abused him. He changed into shorts and lay on the bed. He checked his WhatsApp messages and chatted with me for a while. He told me everything in detail and my replies were reduced to laughing emojis. Even before I could reply to his messages, he came up with something new which was quite amusing.

Almost an hour later, he texted Aisha: *What a disgrace Soham is to humanity!*

Aisha: *Hey, don't forget he is my cousin, think twice before you say anything.*
Rohit: *No way he seems to be your cousin. I love you and your parents, but this guy . . . uffffff!*

Aisha:	*Well, leave him. So, how is my baby finding Delhi?*
Rohit:	*Boring! You are on the ground floor in your room and I am here all alone in this guest room. Pune life is much better; we at least get to see each other there.*
Aisha:	*Lol . . . Don't worry, we get our time tomorrow.*
Rohit:	*Yeah, with your cousin?*
Aisha:	*Whatever, by the way, I have a surprise for you, dear.*
Rohit:	*What? Tell me.*
Aisha:	*Hahaha . . . Wait for tomorrow.*
Rohit:	*Ohhh . . . please!*
Aisha:	*Hold on, baby!*
Rohit:	*Alright! Now do one thing, come to my room :p*
Aisha:	*Hahaha . . . shut up!*
Rohit:	*I can't sleep ;)*
Aisha:	*Switch on the mosquito repellent; I know there are a lot of mosquitoes here . . . hahahaha :p*
Rohit:	*Lol . . . alright! I have your photo with me; I'll sleep with it for the time being.*
Aisha:	*Awww . . . Sure ;) Okay, now let's sleep; we are going out tomorrow, goodnight and sweet dreams, love you!*
Rohit:	*Ahhhh . . . Soham! Nooooo pleaseeee, I want to live!*
Aisha:	*Lol . . . grow up!*
Rohit:	*Hahaha . . . Okay, goodnight now, love you and miss you like hell.*

"Have you taken a few water bottles?" Aisha's mom asked her when they sat inside the cab.

"Yes, Mom," she replied and the car set off.

This time Rohit sat next to Aisha while Soham was in front with the driver.

"Wow! Your cousin has turned brainy overnight," whispered Rohit into Aisha's ear and laughed over his own statement.

"Ssshhhh!" Aisha whispered back, finger on her lips.

It was 8.00 a.m. when they set off. Soham was directing the driver. Rohit was silent as he was completely unfamiliar with Delhi and its roads.

"Bhaiya, stop here," said Soham and the car came to a halt.

He stepped out of the car and then knocked on Aisha's window. She opened it.

"Okay, I will leave now," he said, with a hand on his sister's face. Turning towards Rohit, he continued, "Take good care of my sister. Just because I am letting her go with you, doesn't mean I'll allow you to mess with her. She is my gem, take care of her."

Rohit didn't understand. He was confused but still nodded. Soham then asked the driver to maintain a low speed. He bid Aisha and Rohit goodbye and wished them a happy and a safe journey. Rohit watched him walk away from them as the car accelerated. Rohit couldn't understand why Soham had made an exit from the plan. He asked Aisha about it.

She said with a smiling face, "This is my surprise, the one I was mentioning yesterday."

"What? I still don't get it," replied Rohit.

Aisha held his arm and resting her head on his shoulder, continued, "Yesterday, when you left the dining room, I could sense that you didn't quite appreciate Soham joining us today." She paused and continued, "I don't have a real brother or a sister and Soham is my only cousin. I share almost everything with him and he listens to whatever I say. So, yesterday after you left, I was talking to him. I told him everything about you; who you are and how I met you and how I fell in love with you. He listened and didn't utter a word. After I was done, he asked me about you in detail. Soham is good at heart, he sensed my love for you and he came up with the idea of pretending to go with us so that my parents don't suspect anything."

Rohit immediately hugged her and kissed her.

"Thank you, Aisha, for making this special! So, this was the surprise you were talking about!"

Aisha smiled and took his hand in hers. Rohit now felt a little bad about misunderstanding Soham's behaviour. Although Soham seemed irritating, he definitely had a good heart and loved his sister. Rohit felt guilty about abusing him all the time in front of Aisha.

"Where are we going?" asked Rohit after some time.

"Agra," replied Aisha.

"What?"

"Now Shah Jahan built the Taj Mahal in Agra, so we are left with no choice than to pay a visit to Agra," joked Aisha.

Rohit laughed at her joke and she joined in. They soon reached Agra. The driver told them that they would have to walk on their own for a kilometre or two as motorised vehicles weren't allowed beyond that point. Rohit and Aisha stepped out of the car and made their way through the crowd. The Taj Mahal, being a precious monument and one of the seven wonders of the world, had many foreigners visiting to see its majestic and beautiful architecture. The local guide they had hired explained the history of the Taj Mahal. The two explored its interiors and every chamber and room of the exquisite monument. They also clicked a couple of photos after bargaining with a professional photographer. With the colossal Taj Mahal in the background and Rohit standing behind Aisha with his arms around her neck, it was a perfect shot for the photographer.

Everyone knows that the Taj Mahal is a symbol of pure love and affection. No other place could have been a better destination for the two of them to visit. With Aisha resting her head on Rohit's shoulder, the two of them sat on one of the benches; facing the Taj Mahal, fidgeting with each other's hands.

"Let's get married," said Aisha, suddenly.

"Huh?" Rohit looked confused.

He felt as though a thousand-volt current had passed through him. He was stunned for a few moments and after regaining consciousness, he asked, "Are you in your senses?"

"Oh c'mon, we have known each other for more than four years, it's time to take our relationship a step ahead."

"Marriage isn't that easy, Aisha, we need to take our parents' permission; forget mine at least yours," replied Rohit. "Not that I don't want to marry you . . . it is just that we need to seek permission from your parents," he continued.

"That's not a problem, Rohit!" she said. "Don't worry, just say yes"

"You know I would never say no," laughed Rohit.

Aisha was on top of the world. Her face beaming, she hugged Rohit tightly, kissing his cheek.

Life never gives you a second chance. You have to accept whatever it showers upon you. That day the trip had showered them with happiness. Rohit had a choice to reject Aisha's proposal and wait to complete their course, but he decided to accept. There is no such thing as later, believed Aisha, and Rohit too had a similar attitude.

They then visited a few popular spots in Delhi. With a few selfies at India Gate and a couple of updates on Facebook, the two went shopping. Aisha knew Delhi very well and made Rohit fall in love with the place. Though Rohit didn't believe in God, he was compelled to visit the Birla Temple only because Aisha insisted.

"I've heard there is some place called Hauz Khas, aren't we going there?" asked Rohit.

"It is famous for its nightlife and you know we must return home soon," replied Aisha.

On their way back, the two had only one thought in their minds and that was how they were going to open the topic of their marriage with her parents. Rohit was nervous and Aisha, in spite of being afraid deep inside, showed fake confidence through her body language. They kept thinking of the best way possible until they finally arrived at the place where they had dropped Soham. He joined them and they headed home. Soham asked the two about their trip. As Rohit answered him he felt his own respect for Soham growing, as he was the reason behind their trip ending on a buoyant note. On the other hand, Aisha sat quietly as she knew the most difficult phase of their life had just begun. Rohit would return to Pune the next day and that gave the two only a night to let her parents know about their relationship.

***

"Rohit, what time is your flight tomorrow?" asked Aisha's father during dinner.

"Uncle, it is at seven in the morning," replied Rohit, wondering whether it was the right moment to approach the topic they had been waiting for.

"Soham will drop you at the airport," continued Aisha's dad.

Rohit nodded in agreement. After about fifteen minutes, Aisha dared to speak, "Dad, ummm, I wanted to share something; actually, we both wanted to share something . . . ummm," she abruptly stopped and found herself lost for words.

Rohit's heart skipped a few beats. He started sweating out of fear of rejection. With the topic of their marriage coming up, he was afraid not only of losing Aisha, but also of her parents' reaction.

"Dad, I . . . I like . . . someone," continued Aisha,

stammering. "We first became friends and then with time I started liking him, I . . . I want . . . to . . . mmmaar . . ." She stopped to see her father's face. She couldn't gather the courage to utter the word "marry."

Aisha's parents both looked shocked. Her father glanced at Rohit, who was looking away from him. He understood whom Aisha was talking about.

"No, this won't happen in our house," replied Aisha's dad.

He got up, and looking at Rohit, continued, "Tomorrow morning Soham will drop you to the airport."

"Dad!" sniffed Aisha from behind.

"We will talk about this later," he said and left the room. He probably didn't want to discuss the topic in front of Rohit. He wanted time to think. Aisha's mom was in shock as well. Soham wasn't surprised but pretended to be, in front of Aisha's parents.

"See, this is what happens when you decide to tell your parents, they either ignore the topic or give a firm reply and then cut you down," said Rohit to Aisha over the phone, as he lay on his bed.

"They just can't think as we do; a huge generation gap you see!" he continued.

"Don't worry, Rohit, I know my dad; he is not against this; he just doesn't know you well and he is thinking of his daughter's future. He will take some time before he gives his consent for our marriage," she replied.

The next day, all faces were blank at the dining table. Aisha and her mom served Rohit breakfast. Rohit quickly ate, trying to escape the eyes that had turned upon him since the previous night. He felt acutely awkward. After he was done, Soham guided him towards the cab. Before getting in, Rohit thanked Aisha's parents for their kind hospitality for the past few days. He bid them goodbye but didn't dare to make an eye-contact with anyone. On the way to the airport, Rohit didn't utter a single word to Soham. He was thinking of Aisha when his mobile beeped. He had received a text message.

Happy journey, baby; couldn't hug you before you left, I will miss you like hell. I will try to come back early and then probably again go on an overnight Pune Darshan with you . . . hehehehe and yeah! Don't you worry about my parents, I am here to handle them and convince them, just wait for the good news now ;) read the message.

It lifted Rohit's mood instantly. He immediately texted her back and soon, reached the airport. He shook hands with Soham.

"I will try my best, don't worry, Rohit," said Soham and Rohit couldn't hold back from hugging him. Soham hugged him back. After saying goodbye, Rohit set off to Pune.

***

"Any progress?" Rohit asked Aisha over the phone.

"I am trying my best," she said. "What about your parents?" she further asked.

"No use telling them," he replied.

"No, Rohit! I want you to let your parents know about me," she said in a determined voice.

Meeting the Parents

Rohit agreed. I accompanied him to his house. Rohit and his father were poles apart. They both thought and acted in opposite ways and never got around to talking terms. They would often quarrel over the smallest of issues. Rohit's mom would be sandwiched between the two. Rohit didn't like his dad and so, often shared his personal problems with me. Today, he was left with no other option but to confront his father. We both reached his place for lunch. Rohit's mom knew me well and I was quite comfortable at his place.

"Where's Dad?" asked Rohit, resting his head on the couch.

"He is out on some work," said Rohit's mom, offering us water and somewhat surprised by Rohit's question. He had never shown interest in his dad and today when he inquired about him, the question seemed like a bolt from the blue to her.

After a while, she instructed the maid to arrange the table for lunch and we went through a brief conversation. She asked us about our college and our studies.

"Mom, I like a girl," said Rohit, when the topic of friends came up.

"Her name is Aisha," he continued, looking into her eyes.

Sharing such things with your mother is always easier than with your father. Rohit confidently said whatever he wanted to. His mom asked him about Aisha.

"What will your dad say?" she asked Rohit, when he opened up the topic of marriage.

"You convince him, Mom," replied Rohit.

"But . . ." she began and stopped.

"Aunty, she is a very good girl, trust me. She is one in a million," I added.

"Alright, let's see, I will have a word with your dad," Rohit's mom assured him.

Rohit thanked his mom. We both then went to his room.

"Let's play FIFA," I suggested and turned on the play station.

***

"I guess the flight has been delayed."

We were waiting for Aisha's arrival and were bored as we had been waiting in the parking area for a long time. I tuned in to one of Pune's best radio stations. We listened to various songs to kill the time.

"There she is!" exclaimed Rohit suddenly and stepped out of the car. I was in the driving seat and turned on the ignition. Rohit had Aisha in his arms. They hugged. Although the two had been away from each other for only a week, it was as if they were meeting after ages. Rohit pecked Aisha's cheeks, making her blush.

"I have good news for you," she said as they both sat in the car and I started driving.

"What?" asked Rohit with his excitement reaching the zenith. He turned back, facing Aisha, who was in the backseat.

"Here, talk to Dad," she said, and handed over the mobile to Rohit.

"Whaaattttt?!" his heart skipped a beat and before he could speak anything further, he heard Aisha's dad's voice at the other end.

"Hello, Dad . . . ah . . . I mean . . . Uncle," said Rohit, biting his tongue and clenching his teeth.

Aisha giggled from behind. Rohit was scared; he couldn't find the words.

"Rohit . . . drop Aisha at the hostel, she must be tired . . . and take care of her," continued Aisha's father over the phone call.

"Yes, uncle," he replied promptly.

"And now both of you concentrate on your studies, I want you two to excel in the post-graduation entrance exam and become good doctors . . . and achieve your dreams in life. Once you are done with that, I hope I get to see you and your parents." There was a long silence and then Aisha's father continued, "To discuss about your future."

Rohit couldn't believe his ears.

"Okay, uncle . . . yeah, uncle . . . no problem, uncle, thank you, uncle," that was all he could say before he was asked to pass the mobile to Aisha.

Rohit was on cloud nine. He immediately hugged me and kissed me in excitement.

"Bloody gay," I shouted and pushed him away, trying to control the car.

Aisha couldn't resist laughing. Rohit was so exhilarated

that he just couldn't hold himself back from jumping on to the back seat. He hugged Aisha. She had made his day. Just the mere thought of getting married to her had invigorated him. They gazed into each other's eyes. I kept my hands on the steering wheel while my eyes peeped at them through the rear-view mirror.

"How did this happen?" Rohit asked Aisha, with his arm around her shoulders.

"I convinced my parents; I told them that you are a good guy and would always keep me happy. Instead of emotional drama, I had simple conversations."

Rohit immediately kissed her on her lips and the conversation ceased. She kissed him back and then continued, "Then there was Soham who convinced my parents saying that he found you to be a nice guy who would take good care of me."

"I just love your cousin," said Rohit.

"But you know, Rohit," continued Aisha on a serious note as she rested her head on Rohit's shoulder, "Dad said that he wants us to study and we have to do that. We have to score well in the exams, get into a good branch for our post-graduation, and then, when we are done, no one would ever stop us from getting married. All my parents want is that you stand on your own feet so that we could be financially self-sufficient and happy; that is what every girl's father dreams of!"

"Yes, we will! It is definitely an easy task," replied Rohit and again placed his lips on hers and pushing her on the seat, he lay on her.

I felt uncomfortable and said, "You assholes! At least wait for some time, we will soon reach home." The two felt embarrassed and laughed at themselves.

CHAPTER 8

In the Blink of an Eye

We succeeded in getting our M.B.B.S. degrees in the first attempt and it felt great. The exams were over and we felt as though we were now free from studies. At the same time, we were doctors. The prefix 'Dr' before our names filled us with immense pride. We were excited and felt as though we were on top of the world. Along with the joy, we were also sad that our college life had come to an end. The happy days we spent together flashed right in front of our eyes, making our hearts weep. Done with the entrance exams, we waited for the results, which were expected online after a few months. There was some sorrow of separation too. The five of us had no clue about where we would end up and whether we would even meet each other again. Although we made many promises, we still feared drifting apart.

Almost a month passed and sure enough, we started missing our college life. Aisha and Rohit had already introduced each other to their parents and were soon going to tie the knot. Initially Rohit's father had opposed it but after he saw the change Aisha had brought in his son's life, it made him think positively about their marriage. Rohit's and Aisha's love for each other had never diminished and was among the rare ones which had lasted for more than five years. To celebrate both families accepting them, they threw us a small party. They were obviously deeply in love and made the perfect couple. Passionate about each other, they had also respected their parents' wishes. Aisha was Rohit's life and Rohit was hers. Often, it happens that lovers wish to get married and parents are against their decision, but in this case, they were blessed to have parents who accepted their choice. They were meant to be together and no one could have ever come in their way. I wished them luck and prayed that no danger ever befell them. I wished God continued to shower happiness upon them, just as He has been doing since they met. Kriti and I were also happy with each other, but we were not ready to think of marriage.

"Let's go shopping," said Aisha, when she met Rohit in CCD.

"What for?" he asked, sipping some coffee.

"There is a December sale going on in the malls," she said, getting up in excitement and pulling Rohit out of CCD.

The two set off to the nearest mall. We had earned a

substantial amount of money during our internship and it was time to blow it up. With a variety of brands coupled with the money in their pockets, they bought a great deal of stuff.

"How's this?" asked Aisha, trying on a black top.

"Sexyyyy!" exclaimed Rohit, in delight.

He immediately pulled her towards him and hugged her tightly. She kissed him on his cheeks and blushed.

"I am waiting for the day we get married," remarked Aisha, as they went past some of the sherwanis displayed on the models. "You will look so good in this one!" she said, pointing towards one.

"And you in this . . ." replied Rohit, smiling and pointing towards a saree.

"I am dying to bring you home. You are my life, my soul and my reason to be happy. Life is incomplete without you; I am incomplete without you. There is no me, when there's no you," he continued, as he embraced her.

Neither of them cared about the people around or what they might think. She linked her hands behind his neck and Rohit held her close by the waist. Both looked into each other's eyes.

"You know, Rohit, I dream of us getting married, you wearing a maroon sherwani and I wearing a red saree. You come with the wedding *baarat*, on a white horse, the drums beating, songs being played, people dancing to the latest tracks, there is happiness everywhere. You come to our wedding *mandap*, get down from your horse and walk towards me. We look into each other's eyes and there is shyness and awkwardness inside us. In spite of having known each other for ages, we still find and feel something different in each other—something which we have never felt before. You say, 'You are looking sexy; the day has come, Aisha, when our dream has come true,' and I blush. *Shehnais* are being played, mantras are chanted, people wish us good luck for our new life, a knot is tied between us— an invisible one. Two bodies—one soul, we have immense love for each other," she said, looking into his eyes and then kissing his cheek.

Rohit held her face with love and said, "How romantic, Aisha!"

He kissed her hand and again the two were lost in each other.

"But you know what, I wake up before I can see the entire dream," she said, laughing.

"The part where you take me home is something which I haven't seen till date," she continued and got a little serious. She looked worried.

"Nothing can stop us from uniting, Aisha. You are mine and will always be. Don't worry, baby," he replied, making Aisha smile.

The two then continued shopping. When they finished, they headed for the mall's exit, when they heard a woman calling out to them.

"Since you two have shopped a lot, there is a special lucky draw contest for you. Please fill this form," said the lady.

Being the month of December and the end of the year, there was a contest for women.

"It's of no use, just a waste of time, they are all fake, let's get going," said Aisha, turning away from the lady.

"Just give it a try!" replied Rohit, catching her hand and stopping her.

"No use, Rohit, you never get anything for free."

"You might get lucky, you never know! Just fill it; it's a nightclub form and who can afford to miss one! Just go for it!" he insisted.

"Alright, only for you, my baby," she replied, smiling, and filled the form.

***

The next day . . .

"Hey, Rohit, there is good news for you, I turned out to be lucky," said Aisha in an excited tone over the phone.

"Ohh really? Good news, so soon?" he laughed

"Ohh please! You and your dirty mind," laughed Aisha.

"I've got the pass for the nightclub," she continued.

"Whoa! Amazing, let's go then!" replied Rohit, excited.

"See I told you, you are lucky, after all you are my wife, you have to be lucky," he continued, laughing.

"Yeah, I am certainly lucky to have you," she replied, blowing him a kiss over the phone.

Then she said, "But it is a pass only for girls for a ladies' night event, so it's of no use, I am throwing it away."

"Don't do that, have you gone crazy? Neha and you can go," Rohit went on, getting up from his couch.

She refused, but Rohit insisted. Finally, she agreed.

***

The following day—15 December 2014

"Oh shit! I am late!" I said to myself, as I rode my bike. I was heading towards the railway station. It was 5.15 p.m. and I was running late. I was to meet Kriti before 5.30 p.m. as she was going home to Hyderabad and would return only after our results. Since I had been busy earlier I wanted to meet Kriti for one last time before she left.

"Hey, where are you?" Kriti asked me over the phone.

"Just a minute away," I said, panting, as I ran onto one of the platforms.

"Hurry up, the train is about to leave," she replied and hung up.

I made my way through the crowd to platform number five. As I heard the announcement of the train's departure and the final call for the passengers, I ran faster and after pushing a couple of people away, I finally saw Kriti peeping out of the door just like Shah Rukh Khan in DDLJ.

"You're late as usual!" she said with frustration.

"Sorry, sorry!" I said, breathlessly.

She looked cute with the frown creasing her forehead. I hugged her immediately and she hugged me back. Kriti would return after the results and so we were definitely going to miss each other. She pecked me on my cheek and said, "Take care! Don't stay out late at night, don't get drunk and dance in some procession where you might get beaten up for your pranks," she said, gently touching my face with her soft hand.

"Yes, madam!" I replied.

She laughed and I smiled. Soon, the train started moving. I hugged her again, giving her a gentle kiss on her lips and soon got off the train. I asked her to call me when she reached Hyderabad. She blew me a flying kiss and kept waving as the train moved farther away. I kept looking in the direction of the train until it faded into the distance. I was definitely going to miss her. I felt somewhat sad, but I immediately controlled my emotions and turned back home.

***

"Cheers!" we said, as our glasses clinked. Rohit and I were sitting on the terrace. Neha and Aisha had already left for the nightclub. Rohit had received a call when the two had left. It was 10.30 p.m. and we drank—not alcohol—coke. Rohit had given up alcohol for Aisha and I was left with no choice but to do the same. The dark sky with the twinkling stars made it a perfect night to hang out with a friend. We looked at the dazzling stars as they shone back at us.

"College days were fun, right?" asked Rohit.

"Of course they were! I am already missing them," I exclaimed.

We remembered almost every precious moment we shared and talked about them.

- The day we met, the day Aisha and Rohit met, how our friendship grew, how Rohit and Aisha fell in love, the day I met Kriti, and how I had proposed to her. We missed the days when we bunked dissection classes and roamed around the college, coming back only when the attendance was taken.

- The days we ran from ongoing lectures, directly to the canteen to have some snacks.

- We missed those cadavers, those Physiology practicals in which we had to prick ourselves for blood, the different pathways we had to memorise in Biochemistry, the Pathology and Microbiology departments, the postings, which were real fun. We missed it all. The Histology slides, which all appeared to be just the same, were no more with us.

We discussed each moment and became nostalgic over some. We chatted until midnight. Rohit then talked about his growing commitment to Aisha, musing over how his love for her had developed.

"She is a gem, Alok, she is one amongst millions. I am missing her this very moment," he continued.

I noticed his expression, seeing his commitment, love, care, and passion for Aisha.

After a long pause, he said, "I need to call her now!" and got up, dialling her number. He started walking to the other end of the terrace.

"Hello . . . Hello . . . Aisha? I can't hear you," said Rohit, raising his voice. He probably couldn't hear anything because of the volume of the music in the nightclub.

After trying for some time, he gave up and came back to sit next to me. We resumed chatting. I turned on some music and we started singing aloud.

"Oh shit! Two missed calls!" exclaimed Rohit, as he glanced at his mobile in between songs.

"Five minutes back from Aisha," he said and dialled her number.

I switched off the song.

"Hello, Aisha! . . . Hello . . . what? Hello?" Rohit sprang up, all of a sudden.

"What is happening? Hello, Aisha, talk to me, are you okay?" Rohit's voice rose. He was tense and now, so was I.

"What is it, Rohit?" I kept asking, interrupting his call.

"Hey, whoever you are, leave her . . . Aisha! Aisha! Talk to me . . . Hello?" Rohit shouted and screamed.

He hurriedly disconnected the call and ran downstairs.

"What is it, Rohit?" I asked, rushing close behind him.

"Something is wrong, Alok! We need to go there," he replied hurriedly, starting the car.

I got in beside him. Anxious, I prayed that nothing was wrong. Rohit was sweating. He was worried and his eyes were tearing up. He drove the car at breakneck speed, not caring who came in his way.

"Nothing can happen to her," he kept murmuring.

"What the hell has happened?" I shouted, going crazy with fear.

"I don't know!" he shouted back. He raced the car and shifted the gears to drive even faster.

"She kept shouting 'Rohit save me; help me . . . come here . . .' there was a lot of background noise—not music but people. She dropped her mobile and then the call got disconnected," Rohit continued in an anxious voice.

Our hands turned numb and we were sweating even though it was the month of December. I dialled Neha's number a couple of times, but she didn't pick up. I called Aisha repeatedly, but even she didn't answer. Our tension was at its peak. Rohit continued to speed. Our car skidded as we took a sharp turn. Rohit didn't take his foot off the accelerator until we finally reached our destination. The car screeched to a sudden stop as Rohit jammed the brakes and stopped the car in the middle of the road. We jumped out and I ran ahead of him. There was a large crowd in front of us. Our hearts hammered with every step we took. As we got closer to the crowd, we feared something bad. We then saw an ambulance and a few police officers. Our heartbeats reached a crescendo with the rush of adrenaline. We then found Neha, who was crying loudly. Rohit looked at her and his pupils dilated. We raced into the crowd, pushing aside almost everyone until we reached the spot. What we saw next stopped us in our tracks in shock. Aisha was sprawled on the ground. She was stabbed in her stomach with a knife and blood was pooling around her. The ward boys, who had arrived in the ambulance, soon wrapped Aisha's body with a white bedsheet. Before we could even figure out what had happened to her, she was rushed into the ambulance on a stretcher. Rohit watched in shock. Then he just collapsed on his knees. I ran towards him.

"Rohit!" I shouted, my voice breaking.

He didn't respond. He kept staring in shock. The noise of the ambulance, the police sirens, people running around, some of them scared, there was chaos all around. We didn't understand what was going on. Rohit was frozen, as if a thunderbolt had hit him.

"Aishaaaaaaa!" He shouted suddenly and burst out into uncontrollable tears. He wailed loudly, calling her name. Tears flowed from my eyes, too. Neha was sobbing. I noticed she had a few bruises on her body. Rohit didn't stop crying.

"Rohit!" I shouted, shaking him by his shoulders. He struck his head on the road and tears kept pouring down his cheeks.

***

Coming back to our senses, we rushed to the hospital. This time, I drove the car and Rohit sat next to me. He couldn't stop crying and neither could Neha.

"Rohit! She will be fine! Don't worry, bro," I said in shaky voice, trying to give him fake assurance.

He burst out into fresh tears. The more I spoke, the more he sobbed. It was hard to believe something terrible had happened to Aisha.

As we reached the hospital, Rohit ran to the emergency ward with Neha and me close behind.

"Sir, control yourself, the patient has been taken to the operation theatre, everything will be fine, don't worry, sir," said the nurse, as Rohit inquired about Aisha.

"Nurse, please let me see her, please let me go in," pleaded Rohit.

"Sir, we can't let you in. Sorry! The operation is going on!" she tried to convince Rohit.

"I am a doctor, please, I beg you; let me see her, ma'am, please! I beg . . . Please! Please! I need to see her once," Rohit went on his knees.

"Rohit control yourself! She will be fine," I said, pulling him away from the door. Eyes swollen from crying, he began breathing heavily as he was out of breath. I offered him water and made him sit. Neha too was in bad condition and her bruises needed attention. I requested a nurse to take a look. Then I tried to get her to calm down. Both Rohit and I still had no idea of what had happened with Aisha. Aisha was very close to me and my heart was heavy. I controlled my tears, as my friends needed my strength at that moment.

"What happened to Aisha? What exactly happened at the nightclub?" Rohit asked Neha, after he regained some composure and was now in a better state.

Neha started crying again. She couldn't control herself. I went and sat next to her and put my arm around her, trying to give her moral support. I wiped off her tears and made her a little comfortable.

"Stop crying, Neha, and please tell us what exactly happened at the nightclub?" I said politely as the nurse attended to her bruises.

She looked into my eyes and then into Rohit's. She took a deep breath and looking towards Rohit, said in teary voice, "Aisha and I were dancing, when she received a call from you."

She again took a deep breath and continued, "She

couldn't hear anything so she went out of the nightclub, while she asked me to wait inside. I waited, but she didn't turn up. I tried calling her but there was no answer. Worried, I decided to go out and check, but there was no sign of her. Assuming that she might have walked towards our car which was parked in a lane nearby, I headed there."

Unable to continue, Neha started sobbing again.

"What happened next, Neha? Don't cry! Tell us," I said, trying to hide my tears and worry. Finally, Neha started talking, a little incoherently.

"I saw three men grabbing Aisha by her arms. One of them held her from behind and pushed her down on the road, while the other got over her. They tore away her clothes and started getting physical with her. She cried but they showed no mercy. When she shouted, they covered her mouth. She tried to retaliate, thrashing her legs and arms, but one of them held her down while the other continued getting more physical with her. I ran towards them, shouting. I tried to pull at the man who lay over her, but the other dragged me and banged my head on the road. I tried my best to fight. Meanwhile, Aisha's mobile buzzed for the second time because of you Rohit and she tried to speak to you, but one of them again pinned her arms down. The other two pushed me, slapping me hard. They returned to Aisha, who tried her best to get rid of the man on top of her. She started screaming and fighting back. She cried in pain, but these men didn't stop. She begged them to let her go, but they forced themselves on her. She screamed and they shut her mouth. I tried getting up again, I tried my best to fight back, but they punched me hard and I fell. Aisha had started bleeding, but she continued to fight back. I cried for help, trying to call out to people but I could find no one. One of the men held me by my arms and pushed me to the ground. He threatened me, saying that after they were done with Aisha they would not spare me. I tried my best to resist. When some people started gathering on the road and when the three of them couldn't stop Aisha from screaming, one of them panicked and in the fraction of a second stabbed her in the abdomen. Before the crowd could reach us, they ran away from Aisha. I got up screaming but they all had left. I went close to Aisha, struggling, as I was also badly bruised. I was horrified to find shards of glass nearby from a broken bottle . . . which was inserted into Aisha's . . ." she burst into fresh tears, then continued, "I covered her naked body with her torn clothes. People gathered around, but no one stepped forward to help. They just kept watching. I lifted Aisha's head, but she had fainted from the excessive loss of blood. I somehow managed to get some cotton from our car and pressed it against her wounds. I cried for help, but no one even moved an inch. I called the ambulance, while someone finally informed the police."

Rohit and I were both stunned. Tears ran down my cheeks, but Rohit didn't respond. He was lost in his own world of pain. His hands turned cold and he began sweating but didn't cry this time as tears just wouldn't flow. He was in a stupor. He looked at one end of the corridor. Then, he fainted.

The blankets of happiness had now changed to gloom;

our giggles were now shrill cries of pain. Yesterday's carefree birds were now caged—tied with chains of helplessness. Nowhere to go, and no idea what to do. We were alone, feeling deserted in a busy corridor. Bruises and wounds would heal but the scars would be permanent. We would never forget this day; rather situations would never allow us to. Pain engulfed us. In the blink of an eye, our lives had changed—we had changed—forever.

Alok's House - 26 August 2015

We were stunned and quiet as tears flowed down Alok's cheeks. We were all in shock.

"How could they do something like this?" asked Varun in frustration and brought his fist down on the table with force.

"This is inhuman!" exclaimed Nikhil.

"They were strangers. Hooligans. It isn't as if they knew Aisha or she knew them. All this happened because they couldn't control their bloody libido," Alok went on, in tears.

I got up and with a heavy heart sat next to him. I patted his shoulder and tried to console him.

Varun offered him some water and we sat in silence.

"What kind of mentality do these rapists have? How can they be so inhuman as to forcefully have sex with a girl and then when they see people approach there, they stab her?" I spoke, almost to myself.

"Disgusting!" exclaimed Varun, as if he read my mind.

"They even inserted a glass bottle through her anus," continued Alok, and again burst into tears.

I was also crying now. Chills ran down my spine. Visualising the whole scene terrified me. The pain and the agony Aisha must have gone through that day tore my heart apart. I felt a raging anger and hatred towards the rapists, enough to kill them a hundred times if they were in front of me.

"What happened next?" asked Nikhil, breaking the silence.

Alok had a sip of water before continuing.

"Rohit regained consciousness after a while. His eyes were swollen and the tears didn't seem to stop. With his heart broken to pieces, he prayed to all the Godly idols he could. He went from temple to temple. He poured his heart out, surrendered himself to God and begged for Aisha's life. She was in the ICU in a critical stage. The doctors feared for the excessive blood loss she had gone through. They were also worried about her damaged genitals. Still, Rohit continued praying and trusted God. He was not religious but that day, he laid down his arms before the Almighty. At the same time, the police were doing their work. The doctors submitted a report stating 'pure signs of sexual molestation and rape' and the police started their investigations. ACP Lokhande was in charge of the case then. They were looking for eyewitnesses, interrogating practically everyone. The case had become critical news on almost all leading news channels. All newspapers carried the news on their front pages. They interviewed us, although we were in no state to answer them.

Soon Aisha's parents arrived from Delhi. They were shattered. They couldn't believe what had happened with their child. Rohit's parents were already there and tried to support Aisha's parents—both emotionally and physically. It was that time when we all expected both the families to be busy with Rohit and Aisha's marriage, until this disaster had struck and all hell broke loose."

"What happened to Aisha?" I asked as I couldn't control myself.

Alok didn't speak for a while. Then, taking a deep breath, he said, "She died!"

His words struck like thunder. We were lost in a void of pain. My heart skipped a beat. The words 'She died' kept echoing inside me for a while.

"She fought for her life for a couple of days but couldn't make it. Doctors tried their best. The ventilator was switched off and there her body lay, numb. The news of her death was a bolt from the blue for us. Rohit couldn't believe it. He continued praying for the miracle which never happened. Aisha's mother fainted and was admitted in the same hospital. Aisha was her parent's only child and with her loss, her father felt defeated. He cried heavily, enough to make Rohit believe in the truth. Rohit's parents stood behind him. They knew the pain their son was going through."

Nikhil was in tears now. He was the toughest amongst us, but that day even he couldn't control himself. Although we didn't know Aisha and Rohit personally, or their families, we could feel the sharp pain in our hearts.

CHAPTER 9

We Want Justice!

ACP Lokhande came with some of his subordinates and interrogated us once more. Rohit and I answered our part, giving him an account of each minute of that day from the time we had received Aisha's call until the time she had been taken to the hospital. I had intimated Kriti of the sad incident that had taken place. She was in shock and returned to Pune immediately. The ACP asked Kriti about her whereabouts when the crime had taken place. After Kriti was done, Neha told the ACP whatever she had told us. Mr. Lokhande wrote down everything, every statement put forth by her.

"Could you see their faces?" ACP Lokhande asked Neha, raising his eyebrows.

"Not that clearly as it was dark and there were no street lights, but I can still remember one face out of the three boys," she replied.

She paused, and then continued confidently, "He was the famous industrialist Shrivastava's son."

"Ajay Shrivastava?" inquired the ACP.

"Yes, sir," Neha went on.

Rohit and I were listening to whatever Neha said.

"Are you sure of what you are saying? You know Mr. Shrivastava is a prominent man and a famous personality. So, think twice before accusing his son," he went on.

Neha firmly said, "I can't forget his face, sir. He was the cruellest amongst the three and he was the one who stabbed Aisha with a knife, when he saw the crowd gathering."

He noted that down.

"Sir, did you get the glass bottles from the crime scene? Ajay's fingerprints must surely be on it," Neha suggested.

"The investigations are going on. Thank you for your time," was all he replied.

He then interrogated Aisha's parents and an FIR was filed against Ajay Shrivastava.

After the interrogations, Soham arrived from Chennai. He had been away on work and hadn't been informed about Aisha's demise until he reached the hospital. He couldn't control his emotions when he saw Rohit and Aisha's parents. He adored his sister and this news was enough to turn his world upside down.

On the other hand, Aisha's dad grieved openly, yearning to see his daughter alive. He poured his heart out to anyone who would listen, perhaps to the Almighty. "I had an angel, Aisha, whose life you have taken away. Since the day she was born, I saw her blossom into a doe-eyed, beautiful, radiant, and sparkling young girl who brought boundless happiness and joy into our lives." Unable to control his emotions, he broke down and started to cry.

***

21 December 2014

Six days had passed since the horrifying incident. It was Rohit's birthday but there was no reason for anyone to celebrate. We didn't even dare to wish him. He was in grief and so were we. Around 1.00 p.m. someone rang the bell. Rohit opened the door and found a delivery boy there.

"We haven't ordered anything," said Rohit.

"I know, sir, here is a gift for you," replied the delivery boy.

"Alright!" said Rohit, and unsmiling, took the gift box in his hand.

He closed the door, kept the box on the table, and sat on the sofa. He felt no urge to open the box. I insisted that he have a look at it. At that moment, all I cared about was to bring a little smile on my friend's face. I knew that an artificial gift cannot replace the death of a beloved one but I hoped for a little change in his life. I gently insisted, with no inkling that it would make things much worse.

Rohit finally opened the gift box and found a black

blazer. There was a birthday note stuck inside. Underneath the blazer was another note. Rohit hesitantly opened it.

He read it aloud, "*Happy Birthday, my love! My heartbeat, you are my everything. You are the most precious person in my life. The closer I am to you, the more I fall in love with you. I used to wonder why my heart never beat for anyone and I kept asking myself why I was single. I got my answer later, because destiny had to bring you into my life and so I never fell in love with anyone, until I saw you. I had been heartbroken once and never thought of trusting anyone but when you entered into my life, everything was proved wrong. You were always sweet as a friend and when you became my boyfriend, you loved me in a way no one could have ever loved a girl. You gave me importance and made a place for me in your life. Whenever you fought with me, you came back strong to love me even more. A guy usually gets frustrated with the mood swings we girls have but you even handled that quite efficiently—you are the best! You are my everything—my soul, my life, my reason to breathe. The way you look at me, the way you hold my hand, kiss me, and hug me—every touch of yours brings a spark into my heart and makes me understand how special I am for you. The way you care for me makes me thank the Almighty for bringing a gem like you into my life. This is your fifth birthday since we met and I wanted to gift you something and make it special. I wasn't thinking of a gift until we went shopping last week. The way you were looking at this black blazer, I knew you wanted it. See! I can read your mind! You must be very happy now, probably on top of the world and I just love to see you smiling. I would do anything for that! Well, wear this blazer at our reception; you will definitely make my sisters jealous.*

I think this is getting a bit too long right? Sorry about that! There are more surprises to come, so hold on until the evening. I don't need to ask you to call me once you receive this gift, for I know you definitely will—so waiting for one . . . hehehe. And yeah! Happy Birthday once again!

Love you . . . Muaahhh!

Your future wife,
Aisha Rohit Jadhav"

Rohit broke down into pieces. Tears rolled down his face. Aisha's gift had worsened the situation. She had written the birthday note, almost a week ago. Rohit wanted to hear her voice over the phone and thank her for her lovely gift, and also plan an evening date with her, but he was helpless. He kept staring at the gift. He was filled with pain and it felt like life had come to a standstill. The words 'Your future wife, Aisha Rohit Jadhav' echoed deep within him. The thought that they were going to marry and that Aisha was going to be his wife had been rudely snatched away, along with his will to live, but he wasn't weak enough to attempt suicide. First of all, he wanted to avenge Aisha's death. He wanted to retaliate against the rapists. Now that he knew that Ajay Shrivastava was behind Aisha's death, he wanted to go after revenge. "It has to be an eye for an eye," he kept saying whenever Neha, Kriti, and I asked him about the steps we should be taking.

Although he thought of vengeance, thoughts of Aisha and the fond memories of our five-some friendship, always kept invading him. His mind was filled with . . .

- *She is not with me.*
- *She is no more.*
- *We were going to get married.*

He could barely sleep and whenever he did manage to doze off, he dreamed of Aisha. Memories of the conversation they had at the shopping mall, when she talked about herself in a red saree and him in a maroon sherwani, made his heart ache in pain. Life was miserable for him, but he kept faith in the police, for they were the only ones who could bring justice for Aisha. He thanked the media for constantly supporting them but at the same time, he kept ranting to himself.

- *Had we not gone shopping, the present would have been different.*
- *Had I not insisted that Aisha fill the lucky draw contest form, the present would have been different.*
- *If I had dropped her and picked her up from the nightclub, the present would have been different.*
- *Had I not called her, she wouldn't have walked out of the nightclub to attend my call; the present would have been different.*

And the if-only would go on and on.

All I could say was, "It wasn't your fault, Rohit, the time wasn't correct. Everything is written and decided by the Almighty, it is His game, His players, His rules, and we have no say in it."

"The Almighty! I never believed in him and now I hate him," he shouted.

"You know, Alok, Aisha always believed in God and what did she get in return? This! Was this what she wanted?" he continued, with tears rolling down his cheeks.

He wiped them off but they didn't stop. He took a deep breath and continued, "She was a gem! She changed me. When I liked her, she made me fall in love with her. When I loved her, she made me committed towards our relationship, until the day we decided to tie the knot. When I lied to her in Goa, she generously forgave me, and she started loving me even more. She motivated me to drop my bad habits. I quit alcohol, I didn't believe in God and she made me have faith in Him, I failed in the exams and she lifted me up. Even when I got confused about my love for her and tried to behave different, she loved me back. She never let her love for me fade. For a girl like her, all God does is take away her life and that too, so brutally?"

He poured his heart out, and the tears wouldn't stop.

"What was her mistake? She never flirted with guys like some other girls do. She never exposed her skin to attract boys. She never bothered anyone, she never hurt anyone and still what she got in return was getting raped? Is this your justice?" he asked the Almighty.

I felt terrible. Rohit's pain made me weep. Hatred towards the three men grew. We cursed them. We wanted justice and we wanted the courts to punish them. Even hanging them wouldn't be enough. We wanted more than that. Maybe rigorous imprisonment where they had to beg for their lives until their last breath, turning them into the cold animals they were.

***

A week had passed since the gruesome incident but there were no developments in bringing the accused to court. The police said that they were trying their best and that they would find the accused soon, but nothing worthwhile seemed to be happening. Media was on the job and kept the fire burning. They constantly approached the police station but the officers had nothing to say to them. Every newspaper had headlines of Aisha. People lit candles and carried out processions and marches for her. On Facebook, Twitter, and other social networking sites, Aisha's case was trending. People, including social activists were hounding the police. The case was now on a fast track. The situation turned critical and the police were compelled to aggressively continue working on the case.

A few days later, the police finally succeeded in catching the three accused and brought them to the police station. Although the media was not informed, we were told about it. Neha, Rohit, and I headed to the police station in one car while Rohit's and Aisha's parents followed in another. I advised Kriti to stay out of it.

On reaching the police station, we were asked to wait outside the cabin while the three accused were seated inside. As Neha was the only one who had seen them and was the one to file a written statement against them, she was called into the cabin. Rohit's temper was at its peak. He wanted to go inside and let loose his rage, destroying the three. I tried my best to control him.

Neha entered the cabin and was asked to sit. The three accused were seated opposite to Neha. Ajay was one of them, while the other two were unknown to her at that point of time. On Neha's statement against Ajay Shrivastava, the police had brought him into custody and had somehow succeeded in finding the other two guys as well.

"So Ms. Neha, please tell us who was the one amongst the three?" asked ACP Lokhande, getting up from his chair.

"Sir, this guy," replied Neha and pointed towards Ajay, with tears rolling down her cheeks.

"How dare you accuse my son? This is impossible! I know my son. You are mistaken," thundered Ajay's father, who was one of the famous industrialists in Pune.

"Are you sure, Neha, that he was the one?" inquired ACP Lokhande, again.

Neha took a deep breath. She replied confidently, "I am sure, sir, he was the one."

ACP Lokhande turned towards Ajay and asked him if he would like to say anything in his defence.

"Sir, I was not there, it is a mistake. I agree I was with Rohan and Suraj, but we had nothing to do with the rape. We were busy dining at Suraj's place," said Ajay, with an innocent face.

The interrogations went on for almost an hour. Neha came out of the cabin. Later, the officer met the two of us individually and tried to reassure us.

***

Days passed and the case finally came to court. We hired L. Mohite, a lawyer, to fight against the three accused. Ajay Shrivastava's father, being a big shot, had hired one of the top lawyers to defend his son. We had confidence in the media and our lawyer assured us that we would win the case.

The judge arrived. Both lawyers were present, along with the accused and took the oath, as we watched and waited.

Mohite began on a promising note, "My Lord, according to evidence put forth, and along with the statements given by some of the eyewitnesses, Mr. Ajay Shrivastava was one of the culprits behind Ms. Aisha's rape. According to one of my clients, Ms. Neha's statement given to the police, Mr. Ajay is the one who murdered her after raping her."

He paused to hand over some papers to the judge, and continued, "Here are the doctors' reports, which state that the marks on Ms. Aisha's body clearly indicate that she was a victim of rape and physical torture."

Mohite then called Ajay into the witness box.

He then began interrogating him, "Mr. Ajay, weren't you there at the nightclub, on the 15th of December?"

Mohite asked Ajay various questions but Ajay kept defending himself by claiming that he and his friends were not even anywhere close to the club on 15 December. He further added that they were at Suraj's place.

Next, ACP Lokhande was called into the witness box.

Both Mohite and the defence lawyer interrogated him and asked him to describe the incident. Many eyewitnesses were called and they claimed seeing a girl being raped. Some of them stated that Ajay, Suraj, and Rohan were the delinquents in the case, while some differed.

Finally, the lawyer defending the accused rapists came forward and called Neha to the witness box.

He questioned her, "What were you doing near the club that day?"

Neha replied firmly, "Aisha and I had received a pass for the club and we were at the ladies night DJ party."

"So you must have danced a lot, may be even had some drinks?" he continued.

"Aisha hated drinking but I had some," replied Neha.

The lawyer turned towards the judge and said, "Point to be noted, my lord." He then asked Neha to describe whatever she had seen and experienced.

After she narrated what she had seen, he continued, "My lord, I can completely agree with Ms. Neha that Ms. Aisha had been raped and even the medical reports suggest the same. I feel extremely sad for the girl, but as stated by Ms. Neha, she had been to the club and even had some drinks. In spite of that, her accusation of my client is totally absurd. There were no streetlights in the area and moreover, she admits that she had a few drinks. So, she could easily be mistaken about seeing my clients."

"I have seen Ajay Shrivastava over there. I can't forget the scene," Neha went on, in a louder voice.

"So, Ms. Neha, can you tell what was Ajay wearing?

What was the colour of his shirt?" The lawyer put up his second question.

"Objection, my lord!" shouted Mohite.

"I can't remember that," replied Neha.

"You don't remember the colour of his shirt? Do you remember his car's number?"

"Objection, my lord! Questions are irrelevant to the case," continued Mohite.

"Objection overruled," stated the judge.

"No," replied Neha to the defence lawyer's question, in a soft voice.

"So, what proof do you have that it was Ajay that night?"

"I saw him," replied Neha in a louder tone.

"That is not enough, you were drunk," the lawyer went on.

Neha looked at me and then turned her eyes towards Rohit. He was in grief but expected the outcome to be in our favour.

"There were glass bottles on the ground. Their fingerprints would be on them. They were taken under custody by ACP Lokhande," Neha said.

It seemed like the case was going our way. ACP Lokhande was called to the witness box again.

"Did you find any glass bottles that day?" asked the defence lawyer.

"I am sorry, sir, but I didn't find any kind of bottle. Ms. Neha is probably imagining the glass bottles," replied the ACP.

Rohit and Neha both shouted in unison. They screamed

at the top of their voices that Mr. Lokhande was lying, but the judge overruled their accusations and asked them to maintain silence. A medical officer was then called into the witness box.

"Sir, a glass bottle had been inserted into her; here are the reports," said the medical officer.

Various eyewitnesses were called into the witness box and asked to describe what they had seen. One of them said in his statement that he had seen three boys at the crime scene while another said he had seen two boys committing the crime. When asked if they were Ajay, Suraj, and Rohan, none were actually sure. A few said that they had seen them, while a few completely declined their presence. The witnesses were questioned about the car in which Ajay, Suraj, and Rohan had come.

"It was a Mercedes," said one of them.

"I think it was a Skoda," said another.

Finally, Neha was called back into the witness box. The defence lawyer asked her some more questions. She was also asked about the car.

"I am not really sure of the car. I think it was a Skoda Superb," said Neha, trying to recall the car.

"Do you remember its number?"

"Mmmmmm . . . I think it was MH-12 FZ 3**2."

"Well, my Lord, none of the eyewitnesses are sure whether my clients Ajay, Suraj, and Rohan were present at the crime scene. Let me tell you, sir, none of my clients have a Mercedes or a Skoda. Ajay has an Audi, Suraj has a Maruti Suzuki Swift, while Rohan has a Honda City," said the defence lawyer. He paused to submit some papers to the judge and continued, "Here are the details of the cars."

With none of the eyewitnesses sure of anything, the case became even more complicated.

The defence lawyer then asked Neha, "So, Ms. Neha, when did you leave from the place?"

"I don't remember the exact time, could have been around 11.45 p.m." replied Neha.

"Point to be noted, my lord!" went on the defence lawyer.

He asked Neha to leave and continued, "As per Ms. Neha's statement, she left the place in search of Ms. Aisha at around 11.45 p.m. So, this makes it clear that the crime must have occurred somewhere between 11.30 and 12."

Ajay, Rohan, and Suraj were called to the witness box.

"Where were you that day?" asked Mohite.

"Sir, we were busy dining at Suraj's place," replied Ajay.

"At what time?" went on Mohite.

"Must be around 11.30 p.m."

"Why so late?"

"Suraj's parents were out of station and so we had been boozing at his place."

The defence lawyer then came in. He said, "My clients had ordered some food for the night and here is the bill."

He handed over the bill to the judge and continued, "The delivery of the food was expected to be around 11.00 p.m. which actually got delayed by about twenty minutes. The date and time of delivery is on the bill."

He continued, "To double-check this, I have the delivery boy over here."

The delivery boy was called in. He seemed to be scared as he was in court for the first time in his life and also because it was a murder case. His legs trembled with fear.

"Yes, sir! *Maine hi parcel ki delivery ki thi unke ghar, karib 11.30 baje* (I had delivered the parcel at their place; around 11.30 p.m.)"

The variety of statements given by various people made it difficult for the judge to reach a conclusion. Each person had a different story to tell. The missing glass bottle and the delivery boy confirming that he had delivered the food parcel at Suraj's place had worsened the situation for everybody.

***

Days passed. Forty-five days, to be precise. While we attended the court sessions, we were otherwise helpless. Everything seemed to be inconclusive. There were times when we dominated the defence, while at other times, things seemed in their favour. I believed in God and had hopes that He would definitely bring us justice. Rohit's attitude towards God was pure disgust.

The final day of verdict came and we all reached the court before the scheduled time. I laid my head in front of the Almighty before the court case resumed. Neha looked nervous and afraid.

The defence lawyer again called in the eyewitnesses. Almost all of them now appeared to be backing out. They said they weren't sure of what they had seen that day.

"Bribed! No wonder they are turning hostile!" exclaimed Rohit, angrily. He banged his fist on his thigh in frustration.

Soon, Neha was called to the witness box. The defence lawyer asked her the same questions. She didn't respond. She was in tears.

The lawyer from the defence side again asked her, "Can you describe the scene for the second time? Are you sure that the culprit was none other than Ajay?"

Neha remained silent. She continued to cry.

"C'mon, Ms. Neha, answer!" continued the lawyer.

"Tell him, Neha!" shouted Rohit from the crowd. He shouted until the judge warned him to maintain silence.

Neha looked at Rohit, then at Aisha's parents. She closed her eyes and then opened them. She looked at Ajay, Suraj, and Rohan.

She then took a deep breath and said in a low voice, "No, I am not sure whether it was Ajay or someone else."

"Why you do think so?" asked the defence lawyer.

"There were no lights around and I couldn't figure out who the person really was, I am not sure," she continued, tears rolling down her cheeks.

"Ms. Neha, if you are under any kind of pressure, please let us know," said the judge.

"No, sir, I am really not sure. I did think it was Ajay, but then when I pondered upon it, I did realise I was making a mistake," replied Neha, with a blank face.

"Are you sure, Ms. Neha?" asked the judge. "This might very well go against you," he continued.

"Yes, my lord! I am sure; I don't want an innocent to be punished."

"Everything is fixed!" shouted Rohit in anger, with tears in his eyes. He was out of control. I had to pull him out of the courtroom. Aisha's parents just wept. They cried their hearts out for justice but nothing was happening. The strange thing was, even our own lawyer didn't seem to be interested to push the case from our side with new evidence. He seemed to have given up.

After some time, Rohit, Kriti, and I went inside to hear the final verdict. The judge said, "Mr. Ajay Shrivastava, Mr. Suraj Dixit, and Mr. Rohan Khanna were accused for rape and murder under IPC section B54A, 354B. However, due to the changed statements and lack of enough evidence, the court has come to the conclusion that Mr. Ajay Shrivastava, Mr. Suraj Dixit, and Mr. Rohan Khanna cannot be held guilty and all accusations put forth against them are hereby turned down, setting the accused free. The case is dismissed, thank you."

We were thunderstruck. Rohit fell on his knees while Aisha's parents were shocked in disbelief. Kriti and I couldn't accept that we had been defeated in all ways, physically, mentally, and emotionally. Ajay, Suraj, and Rohan were rejoicing and looked victorious. Their parents embraced them and thanked their lawyer a million times. They were jubilant over the judge's decision. All we wanted was justice, but we couldn't get even that!

Alok's House

Alok was again in tears. Varun patted him on his back. It was 11.00 p.m. We had been together for five hours, discussing Rohit's life, even though we knew neither him nor Alok personally. We hadn't even seen Aisha but we all felt the pain, the agony, and the trouble they had all faced and it seemed as if our hearts would shatter into pieces. I am a short-tempered person and that helped me in working up my anger. I too felt like taking revenge, just like Rohit might have intended to, but one question kept troubling me and that was: why had Neha changed her statement? And that too, so unexpectedly?

I was going to ask Alok about it, when Varun put forth the question as if he had read my mind.

Alok took a deep breath and rested his head on the sofa. He looked at us from the corner of his eyes and said, "Even Rohit, Kriti, and I were disturbed by what had happened. After the court session ended, we stopped Neha in the corridor. She didn't want to talk to us and walked away. Frustrated, Rohit grabbed her by her arm and pulled her towards him.

Rohit was furious with her and demanded an answer, asking her why she changed her statement.

She was crying and avoiding looking at us. Finally, I tried to make her comfortable by asking her to sit on one of the benches. Kriti put her arm around Neha. I tried to control Rohit, who was indignant and impatient.

Finally, Neha told us that about two days before the final

day of the court case, Ajay, Suraj and Rohan had stopped her on her way to the market. It was 7.00 p.m. and she was all alone on the street. Suraj pulled her by her arms, while Ajay and Rohan threw a glass bottle at her feet.

"I was terrified, I thought they would kill me," Neha told us.

They later threatened her, asking her to change her statement against them or else the next time the bottle would contain acid and not water. Neha was petrified. We tried to relax her. Even Rohit's temper simmered down. She kept apologising for what she had said in court. She wept but we knew that she had been compelled to do so. Rohit also cared for Neha.

"Don't worry, Neha. We will fight back in some other way," he said.

Alok then stopped and drank a glass of water.

One night, one mistake, three ruthless people, and many lives devastated, I felt and I am sure Nikhil and Varun felt the same.

"So, what did you do next?" Nikhil asked Alok.

"I did recommend appealing in the high court but Rohit didn't believe in the courts anymore. He said it was of no use, just a waste of energy, patience, money, and time," replied Alok, leaning on the arms of the sofa.

"What happened to the other eye witnesses? Why did they change their statements?" I asked Alok.

"Maybe they were also threatened or bribed. Ajay's father is a rich industrialist and Rohan's father is one of the top businessmen. So money is no issue," replied Alok.

"Money definitely talks!" I exclaimed.

We felt sorry for everyone involved in the case. Rage against the three devils had reached the zenith. They were such evil minds that they didn't repent for what they had done. In fact, to hide one crime, they were ready to spill acid on someone. They had to be definitely punished! Not once but a hundred times!

CHAPTER 10

I Want You Back!

On one hand, we had lost Aisha and on the other, we had lost faith in our judicial system. Everyone had been bribed. Even ACP Lokhande was victim to the green paper, for he didn't mention the glass bottle that he surely would have seen at the crime scene or might even have taken under his custody.

Rohit had been devastated in every way possible. He was the kind of guy who always paid attention to his appearance, but now none of that mattered to him. He kept opening Aisha's gift box and stroked the black blazer that his love had gifted him and then the tears would flow. He would hold the blazer in his arms and weep, saying, "I will fight for justice, Aisha! I don't care if the courts do it or not, all I know is you were my precious gem and those three bastards who hurt you have to be punished. I will fight for justice! I will . . ."

He would wear the blazer and then take it off again, keeping it back in the box. He would cry and this made me feel emotionally weak.

He would then sit by the window, unshaven, looking at the sky. When he checked his contact list on his mobile, the first name displayed was Aisha's, which would make him cry even more. Often, he would look at Aisha's photo and would begin singing the song he had composed.

When I saw you first, I soared up into the sky.
My dreams with you were flying high,
I don't know baby how, when, and why,
But everything happened in the blink of an eye . . .

Then the tears would flow. Her melodious voice constantly echoed in his brain sending triggers of pain through him. He was sitting on the same sofa, recalling how Aisha had been sitting just next to him, when he had strummed his guitar, singing to her. It was hard to believe that everything had happened just a few days ago.

Looking at your cute face I missed my beat,
Beautiful eyes with pink cheeks,
you made me forget what to speak.
'Found my angel' I said with a sigh,
Yes! It happened in the blink of an eye

With Aisha's photo in his hand, Rohit yearned for her reply. He missed her smile, her blush, and her reaction when he had sung this song to her.

> **One look of yours makes my day,**
> **And I wonder what to say.**
> **The way you smile makes me fly,**
> **Yeah . . . It all happened in the blink of an eye.**

The hand that had held Rohit's was now missing. The sofa, the guitar, and everything else were the same, yet everything had changed. There was no Aisha.

> **I then decided you were the one,**
> **And made you mine like a moon for the sun.**
> **We'll be the best and rise up high,**
> **Because it all happened in the blink of an eye.**

He missed her cheerful face, her cute smile, her soft touch, her childlike demeanour, the way she looked into his eyes, and the way she made his heart skip a beat. She would shout at him when she found his room in a mess. He missed this; he missed her arguments, her love, and her care.

There seemed no end to the torment we all were going through.

"We will fight back, Rohit! Let's file a case in the high court," I suggested again. We all longed for justice—and Rohit, most of all.

"No use, Alok!" that's all he said, again and again.

Days passed but neither of us could carry on with life. For Rohit, sleep was out of the question. Aisha filled his dreams and he would replay the dreadful event repeatedly. Each time, one thought that would strike him was this: *Aisha is no more with me, she deserves justice but the criminals are free and leading normal lives. How unfair!*

Meanwhile, Kriti and Neha returned home and only Rohit and I were left in Pune, feeling rather helpless.

***

The day came when our exam results were due. We went online to enter our exam seat numbers and got our marks. Aisha and Rohit had both scored well enough to get admission in the government college of their choice. Aisha's love and struggle in forcing Rohit to work hard and study for the entrance exams had proved to be a success.

"I was nothing, Alok! This girl slogged to get a guy like me to succeed in the exam. She taught me every chapter of life! She converted a non-studious guy into a studious one! Look at my marks! Did I deserve to be here?" Rohit questioned me, with teary eyes and a brittle voice.

I had no answer to his questions. I could only try to console him, but all he did was look at Aisha's photo and talk to her.

He would say, "Why did you love me so much, Aisha? Why? I cannot live without you even for a single second. Why did you care for me? Why did you make a place in my heart that in spite of opening all my heart doors, you don't seem to make an exit? I try to forget you but I can't! I fight to bring you justice, but I can't! I try to lead a new life but I can't! My heart weeps for you, the precious moments we spent together, the love we showed each other, and for the smallest things we did together. Why can't I just leave everything behind? I can't live in the present nor can I think of my future, all I do is go back into the past and keep thinking of you. I keep looking at your photos, talking to you knowing that you can't reply. I keep wearing your blazer but can't even thank you for the birthday gift. My love for you can never fade. Its depth expands with every heartbeat. I want you back, Aisha! I want you. My heart yearns for you, please come back!"

CHAPTER 11

Payback Time!

"Where are you going?" I asked Rohit, when I saw him walking to the main door.

"It is payback time, Alok!" he replied

"Payback?"

"Yes! The court doesn't want to punish the rapists. The only option now is to take the law into my own hands," he replied firmly.

"Are you crazy?" I shouted, running after him.

I tried to stop him and convince him, but my pleas fell on deaf ears. He was focused on just one thing: revenge.

It was 4.30 p.m. when Rohit got into his car and drove off. I tried to follow him on my bike. He was going at full speed and it became difficult to keep up with him. At some point I lost him and had to return home.

He drove to Koregaon Park. He knew where Rohan Khanna lived and so made up his mind to begin his revenge with an 'R' (Rohan). He reached Rohan's place at around 5.15 p.m. He didn't care who else was in the house and planned to directly barge in. Once he got there, he banged on the front door. Rohan opened it. Rohit could no longer control his anger. He grabbed Rohan by his neck and shoved him against the wall.

"What is this?" Rohan tried to ask.

"Revenge!" replied Rohit and kicked the door shut.

He pulled Rohan towards the bedroom.

There was no one in the house, and this gave Rohit an advantage.

"Why did you kill her?" Rohit asked Rohan, in an angry tone.

Rohan was frightened. He didn't even try to retaliate. Rohit punched him hard on his face and hit his head against the wall. Rohan began to bleed but Rohit didn't care. He banged Rohan against the mirror until the glass shattered on his face.

"Please! Please! Don't hit me," cried Rohan.

"Please?" shouted the angry Rohit.

"You want me to let you go?" he kept shouting and brought a chair down on his head.

"Beg for help, shout for your life! That's what I want. Every cry for help that falls on my ears will give me more pleasure in killing you," he continued.

He pushed Rohan onto the chair. Then he tied his hands to the arms of the chair with a rope.

"Even Aisha shouted! Even she cried for her life! Even she was in pain! She was also a human being! She fought for her life and you kept torturing her while entertaining yourself," shouted Rohit, with tears rolling down his cheeks and punching Rohan on his face until he started bleeding profusely.

"That day, she cried and you all laughed. Now it's time for you all to cry and for me to laugh," continued Rohit.

"I am sorry. I was present there but Ajay was the one who started it, believe me! I am sorry. Please let me go!" pleaded Rohan.

"Suraj and Ajay are next on my list. Don't worry! I won't spare them," replied Rohit, with a wicked smile on his face and stopped punching him.

He paused and looked around; then turned back to Rohan. He instructed him to call Suraj and tell him to arrive at 11 E-Street in the next fifteen minutes. Rohan did as he was told and did not mention what was happening at his place.

After making the call, Rohan pleaded, "I have done what you instructed me to do, now please don't kill me, I beg you. I am sorry, I was wrong!"

"Sorry! Ha! Don't say sorry to me," replied Rohit.

"I will say to the person you want me to—even to Aisha's parents, I will admit my crime in court. I'll do whatever you say."

Rohit took a deep breath and said, "Say sorry to Aisha!"

He pulled out the knife hidden under his belt and pierced Rohan's abdomen.

"Ahh . . ." cried Rohan in pain but with every scream, Rohit stabbed him multiple times. He twisted it in his intestine.

There was blood all over the place. With every stroke of his knife, the heinous character of Rohit came up. Rohit shouted "Aisha!" each time his knife made contact with Rohan's body. The impact was fatal and Rohit, lost in his tears and in his own agony, hardly noticed that Rohan had turned cold and continued stabbing with his knife.

After a while, he washed the blood from his knife and his gloves, watching it make its way through the sink into the drain. He later searched through a few drawers, found a gun, and took it. He then picked up Rohan's mobile and without leaving any clue behind, made his way to 11-E Street. In fifteen minutes, he was there. He saw a black Maruti Suzuki Swift car parked under a tree, where Rohan had asked Suraj to wait. Rohit ran towards the car. Suraj saw him on his rear-view mirror, but didn't feel it necessary to step out of the car. Seconds later, Rohit knocked on the glass. Suraj slid it open and arrogantly questioned Rohit, "What? What do you want?"

Rohit was quiet for a while. Then, asking him to open the door, got into the car.

"What is it? Be quick, I have got some work," continued Suraj.

"Nothing!" replied Rohit, with a smirk. He made sure that all the window glasses were up. Then, in almost a split second, drew the gun and pointed it at Suraj. Before Suraj could even react, he pulled the trigger and the bullet travelled its journey across Suraj's brain. He was shot dead, point-blank with his skull being chipped off. The blood splattered all over the glass and the seat covers turned red, as Suraj's body slumped.

Rohit immediately picked up Suraj's phone from the dashboard and swiftly made his way back to our flat. He realised that he forgot the gun in the car, but returning to the crime scene would have been suicide, so without a second thought he reached home.

***

Rohit's parents would often call him and would ask him to return home. Rohit would decline each time, stating that he had important work to accomplish and also that he found peace in our rented flat. College was over but he didn't want to leave the flat. There was no reason for him to stay there but all he said was that the flat had fond memories of Aisha and that he wanted to hold on to them. My parents asked me to return to Satara, but I felt I must stay back with Rohit and try and support him.

Rohit described what had happened at Rohan's place in great detail and how he had killed both Rohan and Suraj. I didn't think it was right to support Rohit over this issue and kept telling him how wrong this was and how it could only doom his future for him, but he hardly listened.

On one hand, I feared for Rohit being arrested by the

police and on the other, I feared being forced into the crime case. As Rohit's close friend and his room partner, it was natural that accusations might be directed against me. If Rohit was pulled to court, it would affect him and even me to a large extent. I was from a middle-class family and my degree and my family meant a lot to me. If any charges were made against me it would be enough to defame me and ruin my life, as well as my family's. I felt like returning to Satara, far from Rohit and his crimes. I did not want to be forced into a police case. The news channels and newspapers had the two murder cases in their top headlines. The police had actively embarked on their investigation. This added fuel to the fire and made the situation worse for me. I feared for my life but I also felt for my dear friend whom I didn't want to abandon. I couldn't make up my mind.

One day, as I contemplated the situation yet again, Rohit approached me and asked me to leave the flat and return to Satara. I refused but he insisted. He probably sensed my dilemma.

"You have to go, Alok!" he said.

"With the two murders I have already committed, I don't know what my future will be. I am likely to be caught, but I want your life to be fruitful. I don't want to ruin your life and the farther away you go from me, the better for you. It has been two days since I murdered the two of them and the police are vigorously looking for the culprit. Your family needs you and it is better that you go back to them."

That brought mixed feelings in me. I prayed both of us had a bright future and that even Rohit would stay free from a police case. However, the situation created by the ongoing media and the police working on the case seemed to make it worse for Rohit and even for me to some extent.

"I know it's a tough call for you, Alok, but you have to go. Aisha is no more; my life is ruined and I think there's still more to come. There's Ajay whom I am not going to leave, which means one more murder soon and that would definitely turn me into a criminal—a wanted one!" he continued.

Tears rolled down my cheeks and even Rohit got emotional.

"I can't leave you," I said, thinking for a while and making up my mind.

"You may not leave me, but I can't afford to carry you along with me," he replied.

"Just go!" he shouted.

Naturally, our hearts wept. Five-and-a-half years of true friendship bound us close. It was difficult for him to let me go and ask me to go away from his life, but it was even more difficult for me to leave him. Finally, we had to reach a conclusion. With a heavy heart, I gathered my belongings. He helped me pack my bags. Later, I copied all the photos from his laptop into mine. Those had fond memories of us—Rohit, Aisha, Kriti, Neha, and me. It made me sob even more. After we were done with everything, Rohit made a last cup of coffee for me and we chatted for what seemed like the last time.

"I'll come back next week, only to meet you," I said as I made my way to the main door.

"No, you're not coming to meet me, nor are you ever going to call me. Please delete all my contact numbers. Never try to get in touch with me, forget me and get on with your life. If the situation turns good for me in the future, I will contact you and if not, then probably . . ." he broke off, his voice cracking. He took a deep breath and continued, "Then probably this is the last time we are meeting."

We tearfully hugged each other goodbye. The day had come where I had no choice but to leave my best friend and go away from him. A friend I had first met in the hostel room; a friend who became my best friend; a friend who became the backbone of my life; a friend with whom I shared my heart, my feelings, my thoughts; a friend with whom I laughed, cried, woke up, studied, failed, passed, cracked rubbish jokes, fought, teased, abused. A friend who was everything for me since the last five-and-a-half years and now, everything was going to change.

***

Alok's House

"Our friendship didn't fade; I still have Rohit in my heart and in my thoughts. I remember him in every activity that I carry out. I want to talk to him but I can't, I am helpless," Alok expressed his feelings to us.

"Yes, friendship doesn't end," added Varun.

We were quiet for some time. It was almost midnight. Nikhil looked at me, indicating that it was late and we should leave. We were about to do so when Alok went on, "Later, I shifted to Satara. I would keep thinking of Rohit. I wanted to talk to him. I would dial his number, but he would never pick up. Many times, it hurt me. I would forget that whatever he was doing was for my own good. Staying away from him would keep me away from the police inquiries. He was doing it for my benefit."

Respect for Rohit had grown in those few hours. Although he was a criminal, somewhere in my heart I had a soft corner for him. After all, circumstances had led to what he had done. Nikhil and Varun probably felt the same way.

"What happened next?" I asked Alok. Although it was very late, I just had to know.

"I don't know! Rohit never contacted me. Whenever I tried to reach him, my efforts were futile. I tried my level best to keep myself updated and always tried to keep a check on him. I had no clue of Rohit's whereabouts until the news flashed that the police had caught him for murdering four people. I immediately made my way to the police station but none of the officers allowed me to meet him," replied Alok.

He paused for a few seconds and went on, "I was then called by Mr. Deshmukh, the officer incharge, for a few inquiries. He interrogated me about Rohit and how I knew him. He has been recently transferred in place of ACP Lokhande, so he knows very little about the case."

Alok had told us almost everything in detail. He then showed us few photos of his college life. We saw Rohit, Aisha, Kriti, and Neha for the first time. My heart wept for Aisha. We felt sad that she was no more. Rohit's better half could be easily seen through his expressions. We could sense happiness, innocence, love, and high spirituality through his photos. I felt terrible for all five of them.

"Is this the same house where you all lived together?" I asked.

"Yes," replied Alok and added, pointing towards a room towards the right, "That was Rohit and Aisha's room."

His revelation sent a current down our spines. The walls of the room had been witness to their happiness. They had seen the two of them bloom and grow, and their carefree, immature past. Now, the same walls of the room seemed to weep in pain. It was as though their happiness had been caged forever.

I ran my hands over the handle of the door, then the white walls of the room, and lastly the chair covered in dust, knowing that Aisha and Rohit must have touched the same articles. The guitar on the wall reminded me of the song Rohit had composed for Aisha. 'In the blink of an eye' he had met her, 'in the blink of an eye' they had fallen for each other, and 'in the blink of an eye' they had been brutally separated. The song just kept resonating in my mind, making it difficult for me to be in the room any longer. I quickly made an exit.

We finally thanked Alok for his precious time and for sharing their priceless past with us. He thanked us for having shown interest in their lives. He then bid us goodbye as we climbed down the stairs.

CHAPTER 12

Finally, We See Rohit!

A month later . . .

We waited for almost a month until we could again make our way to the police station. Varun had once again succeeded in fixing up a meeting with ACP. Mr. Deshmukh.

The ACP called one of his subordinates and asked him to guide us to Rohit's cell. We walked through various passages until we reached the last cell in the row. We saw a man looking at the window. A ray of light entered through a small slit, illuminating the dark room and creating a pool of light in the centre. The man was sitting in a corner, gazing at the slit through which the light entered. It created a shadow larger than the actual size of his body.

"Ro-Rohit?" I called out to him.

He responded to my third attempt. Meanwhile, the policeman unlocked the door and let us in. Rohit looked at us. His appearance was unkempt with his overgrown hair and unshaven beard. His eyes were swollen and drooped, indicating his lack of sleep. His feet and hands had turned black from the dirt in the cell and his clothes were filthy, as if they hadn't been washed for ages.

I was all keyed up. I had to ask Rohit about Aisha, but I just couldn't figure out where to start.

"Rohit, ahh . . . mm we wanted to talk to you. My name is Varun," Varun broke the silence.

"He is Aditya and this is Nikhil," continued Varun, introducing us.

"We recently met Alok and he told us your story. We feel terrible about what happened. We wanted to talk to you," added Nikhil.

The moment he heard the name Alok, he turned to us. He instantly replied, "I don't want to talk about it."

"Rohit! Alok told us everything that happened with Aisha. I know how one bad day changed everyone's life," I went on.

He looked at me but didn't respond.

"I am Aditya, a writer and an M.B.B.S student. I want to write about what happened and I need your permission. Probably my writing about this might help bring a change in society and might save many other girls like Aisha from falling prey to sexual molestation."

After cajoling and imploring repeatedly, Rohit finally

agreed. He narrated everything from the start including minute incidents that Alok had missed.

"What happened with Ajay?" I questioned Rohit, when he stopped.

"After Alok left, I had a pretty solitary life. My existence had turned into a desolate land, but the anger for the three people who committed the crime didn't wane. Although Rohan and Suraj were no more, my revenge was incomplete as Ajay still roamed freely. I tried my best to bring my revenge into action, but failed. He always succeeded in eluding me. On top of it his house was a hell of a fortress with a lot of security guards around his bungalow," replied Rohit.

"So, what did you do?" asked Varun.

"I waited for a few days. I would call Ajay from random numbers that couldn't be traced and threaten him. He too feared for his life, knowing that his friends were no more. He probably had sleepless nights. He would call me up. He would confess his crime and beg for his life. That made me happy. I wanted him to suffer; I wanted every upcoming minute of his life to be worse than the previous one. I wanted him to turn weak, both physically and mentally and finally lie on his deathbed," replied Rohit, with a smile on his face but with the anger burning in his eyes.

Rohit had definitely turned into a monster. He seemed to have no humanity left in him. Circumstances had changed a warm and good-hearted Rohit into a devil, who now thirsted for blood.

Rohit took a deep breath and continued, "One day, after many threatening calls from me, Ajay tried to offer me money.

He said he would give me as much money as I wished, and all I had to do was leave him alone. He tried to bribe me. He said that Aisha was no more and wouldn't come back into my life. At the same time, he said he felt bad for her and confessed that he had committed the biggest mistake of his life. Although I found the redemption money to be unpleasant, I accepted it over the phone and asked him to meet me at one of the most deserted places in Pune. He was afraid but I assured him that I wouldn't harm him. All he had to do was bring the money. He finally agreed. It was the only way to meet him. Although I had assured him of his safety, I never really meant it. I had merely facilitated my next murder."

Rohit paused and then went on, "As decided, I had to meet him near Katraj. I had called him from Suraj's mobile and that's when it struck me for the first time that this move of mine may just go against me.

What if the police are tracking Suraj's mobile? I felt.

Without a second thought, I threw the mobile on the streets of Swargate and headed to Katraj in an attempt to fool the police in case they had been searching for Suraj's mobile. In Katraj there was a spot that seemed like a no-man's-land, with no passers-by and no cars. I met Ajay and asked him to step out of his car. He refused initially but later on, obliged. He handed me the bag with the money, which I accepted and placed on the ground.

When he was about to leave, I asked him, "Why did you commit the crime?"

He turned towards me and replied in a low voice, stammering, "I-I . . . was . . . attracted towards her."

"What attracted you? Her body?" I went on, raising an eyebrow.

"I-I . . . didn't really . . . mean to hurt her . . . but . . . but . . . I just couldn't control myself," he replied, afraid.

I pushed him hard and he fell on the ground.

"Attractive! If that was all, why did you rape her? Kill her?"

"I didn't intend to . . . I am sorry! Please let me go. I have even given you the money you wanted."

"To hell with your money," I shouted, tears running down my cheeks. Aisha's image came in front of my eyes. Her cries, her pain echoed in my brain. Her words, "Help me, Rohit," that she had said over the phone, made my heart cry. I punched Ajay hard. He tried to retaliate sensing that I was about to kill him. He tried to fight back but I stabbed him with my knife the moment he tried to run away. He stumbled and fell.

"Please, I am sorry," he managed to cry, even though he was bleeding.

"I am sorry, I will confess my crime in court," he went on.

"No need, I had given you a chance."

"That is because of your lawyer Mohite and ACP Lokhande that we were proved innocent. They managed all the evidence."

I was shocked and equally hurt but didn't let him escape.

"You have the money! Please don't kill me. I'll give you more if you want," continued Ajay.

"But I don't have Aisha," I replied.

"You will get someone else," he said with ease.

"Someone else? How dare you say that! She was my soulmate!" I shouted.

"You tore her clothes when she fought back, you friends held her down when she resisted. You forced yourself upon her. You even brutally inserted a bottle inside her," I continued.

"You want to see how it feels?" I shouted. After a prolonged fist war from him, I somehow managed to tie his hands first. Then, tearing off his clothes, I pinned him down and shoved a glass bottle through his anal canal. He cried, but I didn't give up.

"Aaaiiiissshhhhaaa!" I cried, looking up and with one blow broke the bottle into pieces just as he had done with Aisha. Yes, it did injure my hands but the physical pain did not matter to me. It was easily overshadowed by the persistent mental pain.

Ajay bled profusely. I stabbed him a hundred times until his heart stopped and he was dead."

We were all stunned by the cruelty of what we had just heard. I didn't know what to say or how to react. Varun and Nikhil too remained silent. I felt uneasy, being in the murderer's presence. I felt a chill running down my spine; probably my brain was playing games.

"You look frightened. Don't worry, I won't harm you," said Rohit, looking at us.

He then continued, "The next day, I made my way to the court and killed the lawyer, but my revenge still remains incomplete. Before I could kill ACP Lokhande, ACP

Deshmukh succeeded in arresting me. I pleaded with him to let me go, but the officer didn't allow me to escape. My parents visited the police station to get me out of this jail but after knowing that my case was nonbailable, they had to leave, dejected. The case has been in court and the verdict is pending."

Tears filled Rohit's eyes. He wiped them off and continued, "I know even a murder of a murderer is considered a crime and I have to be punished for it. I am ready for the outcome."

We looked at him, but couldn't utter a single word. I was confused about what I should say. I thought it was better to leave and so, we thanked Rohit and the ACP for their time. I wished Rohit all the best for his case and prayed for an outcome that would be lawfully correct.

The court trials of Rohit began and in one of them the judge asked him if he wished to say anything in his defence. Rohit was ready for it. He walked towards the witness box on weak legs and a heavy heart.

He began on a low note, "I won't speak anything in my defence. I am a criminal and I proudly say that. Confused? Okay let me explain." He paused and continued, "When I saw her lifeless, I was numb with unimaginable shock. I could see faces around me with eyes following me, some with curiosity, some moist, some with unbelievable blank expressions too bewildered to fathom what had happened. I saw Soham, Neha, Alok, Kriti, and over them the most important people in Aisha's life . . . her parents who had broken down. Days passed with the boorish police trying to investigate the crime in a disinterested manner. Some of them warned us not to talk about the case with the media, as it would severely affect the case, but their motives were dishonest. They wanted to keep us away from the media to hide their incompetence. The bizarre circus continued throughout the trials, culminating into an astounding judgment, declaring the accused free. The judgment had me literally sinking down on my knees, eyes overflowing with tears, body and soul completely battered. Destiny had delivered Aisha's parents and me another crushing blow and my world collapsed around me once more. She was going to become my wife and that meant the world to me. With the injustice of the judgment and the accused set free, I was in a world of pain. I was left with no choice but to murder them and for this, I hold the corrupt system responsible. I was compelled to take the law into my own hands. One might say move on but have you ever heard or seen a bird fly when its wings have been cut off? I am the body of the bird and Aisha was my wings, she lifted me up every time and helped me fly. Now how do you expect me to fly when I don't have my wings?"

He paused. Then, pointing towards the judge continued, "Your system is responsible for this! Had the accused been put behind bars, none of this would have happened and the situation would have been very different today. You claim I took the wrong path, but can I ask you a question? What would have you done, sir, had something similar occurred with your wife or your daughter and the guilty were set free to rejoice?"

He definitely made the judge think. After a while, Rohit continued, "Whatever is my punishment, please give it to me at the earliest. Whatever is my future, I am ready for it. All I want is for it to be quick. I have committed a crime and I am ready to face the outcome. I have no regrets."

The judge adjourned the court and Rohit was escorted back to the prison. All the way, he kept thinking of Aisha. He had tears in his eyes and his heart wept for her. He mumbled to himself, thinking Aisha could hear him.

"Yaadein ye kabhi mai bhoolu na,
Main toh teri hi khatir hoon ji raha,
Jaaye tu mujhse kitni bhi dur,
Main tere hi khatir hoon ji raha.
Tu jaha bhi hai khush tu rahe,
Main mangu bas yehi ek dua.

Pyaar hai, pagalpan bhi hai,
Tu ho sath mere toh zindagi bhi hai.
Tujhse itna pyaar karte hai jo,
Kaise bhool paaye ab hum woh.

Roya hoon, tujhe chahta bhi hoon,
Lekin paa na saku mai ab tujhe.
Kyu khwabo main bhi milke tujhe,
Lagti hai bas teri mujhko kami.
Hum toh naa bhoola sakte hai ise, batao kyu O khuda,
Kyu inhe paake bhi hum hai inse juda.

Yaadein ye kbhi mai bhooluna,
Main toh tere hi khatir hoon ji raha.
Jaaye tu mujhse kitni bhi dur,
Main toh tere hi khatir hoon ji raha.
Tu jaha bhi hai khush tu rahe,
Main mangu bas yehi ek dua.

Translation:

Memories I just can't let go,
I continue to live for you . . .
No matter how far away you go,
I continue to live for you . . .
Wherever you are, happy you remain,
I keep praying again and again.

I love you and I am mad for you,
My life is to be with you
I love you so much and 'you' is what I cannot get,
Now that you aren't with me, how do I forget?

I am crying for you and I want you,
But I know I can't get you,
In my dreams I keep meeting you,
But still keep missing you,
I just can't forget her, why O' Lord?
She is mine but I am alone, why O' God?

Memories I just can't let go,
I continue to live for you . . .
No matter how far away you go,
I continue to live for you . . .
Wherever you are, happy you remain,
I keep praying again and again."

Epilogue

Dard ki dastaan abhi baki hai,
Mohabbat ka imtehaan abhi baki hai!
Aye khuda tu yuhi sitam na kar,
Mohabbat karne walo ko yuh juda na kar.
Jane wale toh chale gaye, lekar meri jaan,
Zindagi yuh thamb si gayi . . .
Lekin kya kare!
Markar bhi zinda rehna baki hai.

Translation:

There's still pain left in my heart,
And love is yet to stand all the tests!
Oh Lord, please release me
off all the troubles,
She's left, taking away my life,
Now life has come to a standstill . . .
But what should I do?
I am dead and yet compelled to live.

Time flew, and in a couple of months, I successfully wrote everything that Alok and Rohit had narrated to us. No sooner had I completed my novel than we heard that Rohit had been summoned again to the court. Varun, Nikhil, and I managed to reach there in time. We saw Rohit's parents for the first time. His mother was crying while his father tried to console her. Soon, we saw Rohit. That day, I had mixed feelings for him. While I felt he was good at heart, I couldn't help thinking that murder in itself is a crime.

It is difficult to conclude whether Rohit succeeded in doing what he set out to. No doubt he managed to seek his revenge but failed to establish dignity in society. His case is still pending in court.

On the other hand, Alok is pursuing his post-graduation in Paediatrics at one of the finest colleges in Pune. He feels sad for Rohit and remembers Aisha almost every day. Kriti is currently working as a general practitioner in Hyderabad. She is happy with Alok. In spite of being away from each other in terms of distance; their love didn't fade and so they have mutually decided to take their relationship forward. The cards are ready and they are soon going to get married. Neha is still single and is happy the way she is. She is pursuing her post-graduation course in Gynaecology in a college in Delhi. Although the three of them live far away from each other, they continue to remain in contact. The only two people they can't see or reach are Rohit and Aisha.

I met ACP Deshmukh one day just to inquire what he felt about Rohit. All he said was, "Rohit may be good at heart but he shouldn't have taken the law into his own hands. Every country has laws for every crime. Even though he didn't get justice in the sessions court, he could have appealed to the high court. Rohit's fight for a cause was good, but his approach was wrong. Even my heart aches when I see people like Ajay, Rohan, and Suraj spoil our nation's name and dignity. I too wish they are punished for what they did but it has to be as per law and not against the law." He wished me luck for my book and thought it could bring some change in people's mindset.

It took me six months to pen down everything Alok, ACP Deshmukh, and Rohit had narrated. A story which I could summarise only in a sentence 'To love, With love.' Probably loving each other selflessly set them apart!

Nobody is innately bad or evil. Circumstances change people and that is what happened with Rohit. The reason for this change was the one bad incident in his life. Although Rohit sought his vengeance, I cannot support him. His path was wrong and no individual should turn to arms. Fighting against injustice must be non-violent. This book in no way supports violence.

Author's Thoughts, Reader's Verdict!

- Why do crimes like rape occur?
- Why is India amongst the topmost countries where girls are sexually molested?
- Why is India the country where 3 out of 5 guilty are set free?

According to statistics, almost every 10-15 minutes, a girl in some corner of this diverse world falls victim to rape.

- Men can't be wrong!

Every second day we hear news of a girl being raped, sometimes in private and sometimes publicly.

- Still men can't be wrong!

After being raped, a girl is tortured with various equipments till she bleeds to death.

- No chance of men being wrong!

"A girl has no right to wear scanty clothes. She shouldn't expose her skin. The way she moves and her exposed skin can tempt people.

She has no freedom to roam out after 7.00 p.m.," this is what people with low mentality have to say.

- Definitely they can't be wrong!

Even when it is a four-year-old girl, she is the one responsible for being raped by her very own father; her own father can't control his bloody testosterone level from boosting up at the sight of her skin.

- Yes, even the four-year-old girl should have known the low mentality of these men. She should have learnt it when she was in her mother's womb.

The problem with India is not with the girls but the sick mentality of few individuals. It is easy to blame the law and the lack of action taken against the crime. Of course, to an extent you are correct! Laws have to be strict but what is more important is changing the mentality of those who commit the crime. Ask the rapists what they would have they done if something similar happened with their own mother or sister? How would they react?

Nothing is impossible. If we all strive hard together, we can definitely bring change in our society. Every parent who discusses this issue with their children rather than hushing it up could really create wonders. Sex education must be introduced in text books, right from an early stage.

When a girl is raped publicly, people gather around and watch her getting sexually assaulted. If a girl bleeds on the road, the mob will discuss the scene rather than step forward to help the girl. Too many deaths occur because of the delay in getting the victim to the hospital. People pray for the victim, light candles in front of India Gate, protest against the criminals by carrying out rallies—but how does that help? It would be better if the same crowd helps the victim instead of watching her die. What happened with Aisha was exactly this—the people around preferred to be spectators rather than show some compassion!

I support neither Rohit nor the rapists. Both were wrong in their own ways. Just like ACP Lokhande and the lawyer Mohite, many people forget their morals for their personal greed and motives. Laws aren't always wrong but a few people who are responsible for enforcing them are. These same corrupt people might succeed in amassing luxuries in their lives, but can they look into their children's eyes and say at least once that they were on the right path and are true to themselves? Think over it, guys!

Now let's come to the laws!

Before 2013, the maximum punishment of rape in India was only 7 years of imprisonment. After the Nirbhaya case, the Indian Government made amendments in the law, passing the ANTI RAPE BILL, putting rape on the list of serious crimes and extended the 7 years of imprisonment to life imprisonment or death sentence, depending upon the severity of the crime.

So, we do have some good people in the government too!

In Saudi Arabia, irrespective of gender, the guilty is publicly beheaded. China too punishes the rapists with a death penalty by firing a single bullet directed at the spinal cord joining the neck. In most of the cases, the punishment is castration where the guilty male loses the use of his sexual organs. France has more well-defined and extensive laws against rapists. Punishment varies from 20 to 30 years of imprisonment accompanied by torture. This was just a superficial comparison of various laws prevalent in some countries.

How about India? Do we have stringent laws or we need to change them? You decide.

The main aim behind this novel is to bring a change in society. I not only want to see a better India but also a better world. The change has to take root from us. Just like you love your mother, your sister, your friend, your girlfriend, or your wife, it is important to respect all girls. Gandhiji stated:

- Bura mat dekho (Don't see evil)
- Bura mat suno (Don't hear evil)
- Bura mat socho (Don't think evil)

I respect Gandhiji and his thoughts and think that everyone should follow them.

I feel sorry for all the victims of rape and sexual molestation till date. For all those who have lost their lives, we can only pray that their souls rest in peace and that their families attain justice. May God help them in overcoming the agony they are going through!

This book is dedicated to you all!

The Book Says

Thank you, my friend, for choosing me. I hope you enjoyed my company till the very end. For an author, his creation gives him immense pleasure and satisfaction. It would warm my creator's heart and mine, if you could spare a minute and post a review from the portal you purchased the book or upload a picture of me with your response on Facebook or Instagram. Yes, you can pose with me for a picture. I do look beautiful in this cover I wear.

Add **#adityanighhot #untillovesetsusapart**. You can tag the author as well. Your support will help get me more readers.

Thank you and happy reading!

About the Author

Hailing from Pune, Aditya Nighhot is the national bestselling author of four books, a doctor (MD Radiology) by profession, a screenwriter, an entrepreneur, a motivational speaker, and a social media influencer. His books have not only received critical acclaim but have also successfully managed to be in the top 50 best reads and bestsellers on Amazon for months together. Having sold over 50,000 copies of his books, Aditya's work has been translated into Hindi and is about to be published internationally in Sinhalese, German, French, and other languages.

His books *Tagged for Life: Will You Be My Wife?* and *Unhooked & Unbooked* have been declared the 1 and 3 most loved books of the year, respectively, by ANI. His books have won him the 'Best Romance Book of the Year–Readers' Choice Award. MID-DAY, a leading media house. compared the author's success with that of legendary author Mr Amitav Ghosh. *The Global Asian Times,* Toronto (Canada) published an article stating, 'Love not worth dying for proves doctor and author Aditya Nighhot.' Aditya is also among the few authors in India to write chatbot fiction on the Readify app. His book *Unhooked & Unbooked* has made it to the stores with a record-breaking 200 + media mentions in a single day. Aditya is very active on social media and loves interacting with his fans and followers.

On the academic front, Aditya stood 47th in the All India BVP Medical Examination and completed his MBBS from one of India's topmost medical colleges. He is currently pursuing a career in MD Radiodiagnosis. A member of the Screenwriter's Association, Aditya has pursued screenwriting at Ramesh Sippy Academy and is currently working on a few scripts.

As a co-founder of Dreamboat Publishing, Marketing, and Distribution, Aditya and his team have successfully marketed and promoted more than a hundred authors and made their books bestsellers within months of release. A one-stop destination for authors, the company is always open to young talent. It has now opened a new wing that will promote and market not only authors, but also actors, models, influencers, entrepreneurs, companies, startups, etc.

You may get in touch with the author at:

Instagram: @adityanighhot

Facebook Profile: www.facebook.com/authoradityanighhot

Facebook Page: www.facebook.com/adityanighhot

WhatsApp: +91 9623068037

To invite him as a speaker or guest at your college, workplace, or institution and to collaborate with him, you may visit his website or get in touch with his team via email.

Website: www.adityanighhot.com

Emails: contact@adityanighhot.com
aadi9626@gmail.com,
manager@adityanighhot.com

**To buy more books by the author
scan the QR code given below.**